LOVERS CATCH

THE SEA MEN, BOOK 1

DANI STOWE

BABE
FUEL
BOOKS.COM

The Sea Men

∼

Edited by Kim Burger

∼

WARNING: This book contains material that may not be suitable for all readers due to its sexual content, graphic imagery, and some violence.

∼

∼

❦ Created with Vellum

SHELLEY

*T*here's a chill in the air. It's not completely unusual for this time of year, but the wind is making this experience much more uncomfortable than I could've anticipated.

The sky is gray and I'm sure Aunt Cora is up there, above the clouds, waving her cosmic energy around and making this thousand-foot climb up to the top of Lovers Peak more difficult than it should be.

Not to mention, my backpack is heavy on my shoulders, and I wonder how someone who has been reduced to ash can still be so heavy. I sigh feeling foolish about engaging in another one of her silly ventures. Even in death, I can't seem to escape the weight of Aunt Cora's musings.

I don't know why I'm doing this. I feel guilty, I guess. I missed last year's hike with her and then she had to go and die on me. The ol' lady wasn't really even that old—sixty-five —and she left me without any other family, except for the ones in her head and are now stuck in mine.

Merpeople.

For a psychic, Aunt Cora certainly knew how to mess

with my head. She messed with everyone's head. She insisted mermen were real and I'm not sure if I should feel fortunate or not for being the only one who ever believed her.

Men with fishtails—ridiculous!

I remember in high school how I *wanted* mermen to be real, to be true. I blurted about the possibility in defense of Aunt Cora when my classmates would say shit about my crazy aunt. That always proved to be a dumb move. I never had any friends back then.

Now I'm twenty-four and instead of traveling to Europe with my best friend, I'm hiking up to Lovers Peak on the longest day of the year, which is not just the summer solstice, but the day Aunt Cora insists mermaids, or mer*men*, might reveal themselves in the bay below.

I look beyond the edge of the sloping trail I'm traveling. The bay looks peaceful—no waves or signs of life. Unlike the small town beyond the mountain where I grew up, there's no chaos out here, except for the chilly wind blowing about me.

I change my mind. This is *not* usual weather for this time of year. The prickle of the nippy air gives me goosebumps and by this point of my hike, I should be sweating, from what I can remember.

Looking up, I'll have to use my hands to help me with the incline the rest of the way. I never liked this part of the hike. Aunt Cora used to laugh at me about it because I didn't like to get my hands dirty. I still don't, but she insisted I was an "earth child," like my mother. It vexed Aunt Cora because she could never make sense of my aversion to dirt.

Earth, moon, sun, fire, wind, water—I can't believe I used to buy into all that psychic mumbo-jumbo bullshit. And sex! Oh God, the woman could go on for hours preaching about the unification of sexual bodies and the magical elements they produced. I'm surprised I didn't end up more messed up in the head than I am now.

Seriously! Who talks to a five-year-old about sex?

"We shouldn't be ashamed of our sexuality and especially not sex," she used to say. "That's how we are made because it's how two lovers are most deeply connected."

Bullshit! I connected with a bunch of dudes all through college and there was nothing deep about it other than the occasional big guy that would wedge himself too deep to the point it got painful, especially if I turned on my side, throwing one leg over his shoulder.

It's all proof love is just a pain. I've never felt connected to anyone—not in the way Aunt Cora described and, truth be told, I wouldn't want to connect or fall in love anyway.

Love is what killed my parents although I'm not a hundred percent sure exactly how they died and no one in this rinky-dink northern coastal American town has any clue either.

Aunt Cora had a few crazy ideas of her own, but she's gone now, so I'd like to believe she told me stories to comfort me. "They died together," she said of my parents. "One could not go without the other. They were connected, and they chose to stay that way for all eternity."

Connected. What a bunch of crap. I could be wrong though as I feel my butt vibrate. Pulling my phone from my back pocket, I smile when I see who is trying to connect with me right now.

"Hey, what's up?" I ask.

It's Kumiko. She's half Japanese and half Puerto Rican and always seems to be at odds with herself, always trying to figure out her true identity. She blames her mixed heritage. She says there's an eternal, internal argument going on that makes her crazy. She complains rice should not come in so many variations—rolled in seaweed versus soaked in sofrito because it's too hard to choose between the two. Kumiko says it's like choosing between her parents, who are divorced.

Personally, I'd choose both, but I realize Kumiko just likes to argue as her parents still do, despite the fact they don't live together anymore.

Yep, Kumiko is a firecracker, like me. Her long, silky, thick, black hair, which makes me jealous because she never has to fix it, never hides her prominent cheeks or the stark whites of her brown eyes that flare red whenever she's angry. When she's really abashed, you can see her entire body blush under her tan skin.

But I'm white and I'm told my long, wavy, strawberry blonde hair of Celtic origin is what adds to my stubborn temperament. Aunt Cora used to say I had a little fire in me, which I got from my father, and it adds to my occasional sharp tongue. But stabbing people with the snap of nasty words and insults is rare. I owe Aunt Cora for that. Growing up I called her all kinds of nasty things: fat, ugly, a bitch, a demon. That last one she didn't like at all, but each time, instead of spanking me, she'd throw water in my face. She claimed it was the only way she knew how to put out my fire.

"How far are you up the trail?" Kumiko asks on the phone.

I look up. "I'm almost near the top," I say and halt to catch a breath, so I can speak.

"When you reach the peak, don't forget to flip a finger up to your Aunt Cora for me."

I laugh.

"Don't laugh!" Kumiko flares. "I'm sure the old racist bitch is expecting a little something from me, as well."

"She wasn't racist, Kumiko. She loved you. She just had a weird way of showing it."

"I have the only palm in the whole world your Aunt would not touch or read to tell me my future. And I bet I know another reason why. Do you want to know why Shelley?"

I pause my legs to seat my butt on a boulder. "Why?" I ask, although I probably shouldn't have led her on.

"Because *she* knew I'd be able to tell if she was a fraud. That's why."

I'm afraid to tell Kumiko my aunt taught me to read people's hands to tell them their fortunes because I wouldn't read Kumiko either, even if my best friend begged or paid me as some people did for my aunt. I learned when I was young that people didn't pay Aunt Cora to learn their fate. They were really after reassurance or hope, which explains why my aunt typically lied. I'm sure Aunt Cora took one look at Kumiko and, without even reading her hands, put my best friend in the *hopeless* category.

A thunderous *boom* rattles my bones and I nearly drop the phone.

"Holy crap!" shouts Kumiko as I adjust the phone to my ear. "What the hell was that?"

"Thunder." I'm just as surprised as Kumiko. I did not see this coming at all. The weather forecast reported nothing but blue skies.

"Girl, I told you-you should've skipped the hike up Lovers Peak and come to Europe with me. I'm not having a good time without you and now you're going to die of electrocution by lightning."

"Thanks for the support, Kumiko. As if the thunder wasn't scary enough while I'm by myself up here—"

"So, get down!" Kumiko yells. "Get off the damn cliff before you fall. And then get on a plane so you can explore these dark and dirty streets of Europe with me."

"Let's be honest," I say as I look up towards the peak that is collecting gray clouds above. "The only thing you're looking for is foreign European men that might bind you to a dark and dirty hostel bed and screw you. And the only reason you want me there is to make sure they don't murder you, like in that horror flick we watched."

I study the trail to the peak and there are only fifty or so more feet to go. The wind blows a single leaf across the rocks, drifting all alone, like the way I feel right now.

I shout, "And see what you did! I'm by myself and now I'm freaking out feeling alone up here!"

"Oh. C'mon," pleads Kumiko and I'm shaking my head as I look out towards the bay in hopes of calming my nerves. I see something flip out of the water as she continues. "Just because you've never tried a little S&M doesn't mean you won't like it."

"I'm not that kind of girl," I mutter and stand up from the boulder to get a better look at the splash coming from the center of the bay below.

Another *boom* of thunder crashes through my bones and echoes through the crescent of the rocky mountain surrounding the bay.

"Get off the trail," Kumiko says sternly, and I see a creature of some sort wading in the water. I swear it appears to see me, too.

"But there's something out there," I tell her.

"Something out where? What are you talking about?" Kumiko sounds worried.

I appreciate having at least one human being still left in this world that cares about me. "There's something in the bay," I say as I get up from the boulder and go off the trail into a clearing to get a better look.

"Like what? A boat? I thought you said there are no fish in that bay?"

"No, its like an animal of some sort. I can see it jumping in an arch in and out of the water. I almost think its showing off to me."

"Like a dolphin? That's cool, but I can hear the thunder

cracking in the background and I can barely hear you through the wind blowing on your phone."

I pull my hair away from my eyes as the wind blows a few wavy locks into my face. "It's not a dolphin. I can't tell what it is, but it has a giant fishtail and what looks like arms. It's very strange."

"So, it's a fucking octopus!" snaps Kumiko. "Get off the mountain, Shelley, before you get trapped up—"

"Whoa!" I yelp as I feel my foot slip out from under me and I land on my ass with one leg hanging over the cliff.

"What the hell happened?" shouts Kumiko in my phone, but her voice is breaking up.

"I slipped," I admittedly yell and squeeze the phone between my shoulder and ear to dust my hands. I see some dirt mixed with a smear of blood where I scratched my palms.

"See!" Kumiko shouts as another blast of thunder rumbles through the clouds. "You need to get off that trail before it rains and you fall to your death."

Death? "You're probably right," I say as I slip my hands under my butt to get up.

Straightening my knees, I notice the creature is looking at me. Right. At. Me. From the center of the bay. And the thing looks a lot more like a human than a creature. I swallow. "Uh, Kumiko?"

"You okay?" she says, as the connection on the phone line seems to be getting weaker.

My heart is racing. "There's a man staring at me."

"Is he weird? Does he look like a serial killer?"

"No," I whisper. "It's the thing in the water. I'm sure it's a man and it's...or *he's* looking at me."

"From down in the bay?" Kumiko asks. "You're not making any sense."

She's right—I'm not making any sense. *This* doesn't make

sense. I know I saw a fishtail earlier attached to that same figure and now the figure appears to be a man, who's not wearing a single thing over his torso, sticking halfway out of the water up to his waist.

I watch him dive headfirst into the bay. As his bottom comes over the surface, I notice its smoothed over with glimmering blue-green scales that merge into what I swear looks like an enormous fishtail.

"Holy shit, Kumiko!" I shout, adjusting the speaker at my mouth, but my phone slips right out of my hand.

No! I drop to my belly and quickly try to reach for my phone—*falling*—as I hear Kumiko's voice shout my name. But all I can do is watch as my only connection slams into rocks and petrified branches before shattering into hundreds of pieces and finally hitting the water. My heart sinks, as my phone does, too, and I feel the cold sting of a wet raindrop fall onto the back of my thigh right below my shorts.

Fuck. I look up at the sky. It is now covered in a heavy, dark gray blanket of clouds.

I've lost my phone and it's going to rain.

I look out to the bay below. It scares me to think what might be lurking within the cascade of deepening, dark blue waters. It scares me more to think my Aunt might've been telling the truth.

Mermen? Nah. I'm sure it was a dolphin or other sea creature just as Kumiko said...but now I'm freaked out because I'm alone and have no cell phone.

The chill of the air gets colder as more drops of rain collide with my skin. I get up, rubbing my arms and smearing the wet rain over the surface of my skin when curiosity gets the best of me, so I scan the surface of the bay for any signs of life.

From left to right, I search, but... *nothing.*

"Mermen," I chuckle to myself as more rain begins to fall.

Turning towards the trail, I look up towards the peak. "I'm not going to make this trip today, Aunt Cora," I say aloud, tugging on the shoulder pads of my backpack. And, just as I take one step off the path, the clouds open the dams letting rain flood over me and my path.

Great.

I start walking and realize I have no idea what Kumiko's phone number is. Her number was programmed into my phone. I panic. I also have no idea what my flight number is to get back home because that was programmed into my airline app as well.

I tighten my grip over the shoulder pads of my backpack, knowing I still have my wallet and cash. Although, I'm sure it's going to get as soaked as I'm getting right now. I tug some strands of wet hair from eyes, blinking. At least Aunt Cora is dry. I was right to put her ashes in an airtight urn. There's no way I better lose *thaaaaa...!*

My leg slips out from under me again, but this time I go flying through the air, landing on my back. Mud is all around me and I feel like my body is moving. I'm drifting slightly... *No...* I'm sliding!

Clawing my hands into the ground, I try to keep myself from gliding through the thick mud, but my palms sting from the scrapes I suffered earlier, so I quickly shake the mud away. The mud in my hands feel slick and a river of mud begins to flow rapidly about me as the rain continues to fall. Quickly, I realize I'm moving as fast as the mud flowing and I'm beginning to glide downhill. Faster, I go and...

Oh crap! I'm caught in a mudslide...

I can't stop!

I try grabbing onto a tree limb and then a rock, anything to slow me down because I'm picking up speed as I go down the side of the mountain like I'm on some splash roller coaster in an amusement park.

Damn, it hurts!

The sensation of every bumpy, jagged rock and splintery twig hits the inner flesh of my thighs. As I squeeze my legs tight together to stop the torture, other parts of my body become a bullseye for nature—striking against my shins, hipbones, and elbows. I feel useless against the rocky terrain that was once dusty and dry but has trapped me into a downward, spiraling landslip.

I look ahead and see the edge of the mountain and the bay below. I recall how my phone crashed and crumbled into pieces before it finally sank into the bay and I wonder if I will experience the same fate.

I try harder to grab onto the next tree limb, but it snaps. Reaching out to the next small boulder, my muddy hands slip right over it. Still sliding, I try to aim my body towards the next tree trunk, but mud splashes into my eyes and I miss the tree. I quickly wipe the mud away as I pick up more speed with the edge of the cliff just a few yards ahead. I'm panicking worse knowing gravity and velocity are pulling me faster and faster down the mountain.

I finally accept there's no way I'm going to win against these elements—gravity, the mountain, the mud, so there's only one thing left to do—

Scream!

Suddenly, my entire body is hoisted into the air. My stomach wrenches up into my throat as the mountain throws me off its cliff. The mouth of the bay around me widens and I peep down. Below, I see the dark water about to swallow me, so I squeeze my eyes shut.

Landing hard, I crash into the enormous cerulean pool. I immediately try to swim up to the surface, but I can't, as my nose stings from the impact making me dizzy with pain. I push the achy thought out of my mind as I realize I'm sinking. My boots feel heavy and so does my backpack.

Reaching to my waist to unfasten the clips that keep my backpack snug on my back, I remember I broke one end this morning and just knotted the straps around me. As I try to unknot the ends underwater, I notice the infinitely black bottom of the bay and feel my pulse pick up its pace. I extend my hand down to my boots, which feel like concrete pulling me deeper, but it's taking a shit ton of effort to undo the laces. I accidentally open my mouth and swallow some water. Now, my body feels even heavier. The surface is getting farther and farther away as I sink down into the abyss.

I try to swim with every ounce of might I have, but I'm getting tired and not going anywhere. I swallow a little bit more water and notice how the water tastes both clean and dirty at the same time. It's a familiar taste—one I recognize from when I was younger when I played in the bay as a child with my parents. The taste should comfort me but it doesn't because—

I need air!

A rush of adrenaline overcomes me, flooding my body and allowing me to flap my arms and kick my legs as hard as I can to move them as more water seems to be flooding my cavities. Choking, I instinctively try to take a breath, but there's only thick heavy water. It's so weighty I can't feel my muscles or move my legs anymore, but I can still feel my own skin, which feels cold. I feel cold and alone.

I look up one last time knowing I'm about to get lost in darkness. I don't want to see the abyss about to engulf both my body and soul. Between strands of my hair floating about my face, I vaguely see the man I'm sure I saw earlier splashing in the bay. He is now circling above me...

And he *does* have a fishtail.

2

SHELLEY

I think I'm going to be sick.

I roll to my side. Water trapped in my gut is about to burst from my throat, but I'm startled to see sand. I rub my hands through the warm, dry grains beaming under what feels like a hot sun shining above me. I attempt to lift my head to take a peep of my whereabouts, but my body won't let me. I puke.

Water pours out from inside and as it does, I remember I was drowning. I wipe my mouth with the back of my hand, remembering the heavy pull of my boots toward the bottom of the bay. Looking down, I see my boots still tied to my fair legs roasting under the sunshine.

The weight of the shoulder pads from my backpack pull me back flat to the sand. The straps are still tied in a knot around my waist, which feels tight—tighter than it did before. In fact, the straps feel like they're strangling my waist, which is about to explode...

I puke again.

My stomach aches as it squeezes the bay water out of my body, but the whole thing makes me feel better and relieved.

I'm still alive. "Yes, I'm alive," I say aloud to myself to hear confirmation of my existence. I lean over further to hurl again and suddenly the sensation of fingers moves across my cheek and behind my ear, pulling the few strands of wet hair away from my face.

I choke. Someone is right behind me, but I can't look right now. The last bit of water empties from my belly as the fingers transfer to my shoulder and a whole hand, a strong hand that feels like a man's hand, squeezes and then moves to my back to pat me as I start to cough.

Oh fuck. I'm scared to see who it is. I bet it's my rescuer. I don't want to look at him. I'm embarrassed, but at least I'm not nauseous anymore.

My rescuer's hand runs through my hair at the back of my head. It's awkward to be pet by a stranger, but the feeling is comforting at the same time. I'm sure he pulled me out and is trying to be nice by offering more support.

I roll towards my back, propping my backpack under me. The bright sun forces me to squint as a shadow blocks the blinding light and a handsome face comes into view, peering down at me.

Now, I'm really embarrassed.

The face is beautiful. It's framed in thick, messy, shoulder-length black hair that is a stark contrast to eyes that are so blue, both the sea and sky should be jealous. The face of a strong man smiles and the stubble lining his jaw makes him look rugged and sexy. A "wow" escapes my mouth and shame washes over me as I feel my face flush.

He laughs and I'm comforted by the weight of his body, which I hadn't noticed was resting on me. He puts his hand on the side of my head to prop himself above me. As he does, a drop of water falls from the tips of his hair and into my mouth. Tasting the salt water on my tongue, I feel his strong fingers move to the back of my head as he squeezes then massages my neck.

If this is the usual treatment for someone who's been rescued— I'm going to try drowning more often.

I look down at his chest of rippling muscles beneath bronze skin. He must be a lifeguard of some sort. I should probably say thank you at this point, but I'm too distracted by how beautiful he is—half wet and half-naked, except for the antique-looking coin hanging by a golden chain from his neck. The jewelry is as enticing as he is and it makes me more curious and inclined to stare.

Goddamnit! I think the hottest, tannest, and most gorgeous man on the planet just rescued me. *Say something, Shelley!*

I open my mouth to verbalize a word, any word, but all that comes out is a gurgle of leftover water in my throat and I cough hard. I swear I might have spit in his face.

As he rolls off me, I feel foolish. "I'm sorry," I say and he pulls at my chin, forcing me to face him.

The centers of his eyebrows are raised, as though he feels sorry for me and he grins and shrugs. He moves his thumb across my cheek then runs his fingers through my hair once more. I get goosebumps realizing I've never been caressed so much in all my life—at least not since I was a small child.

"Did you save me?" I ask as I cough a little more though I try hard to hold the bay water back.

He grabs the back of my neck once more and makes direct eye contact, setting my insides on fire. I try to contain myself as he smiles and nods and I hear movement at my feet —something's not right.

I glance down and see what looks like a fishtail, except it's not just any fishtail. It's a *ginormous* fishtail the size of an entire dolphin! But unlike a dolphin's smooth, rubbery exterior, *this* tail is covered in disk-like, scales with a glistening turquoise tint.

I stare at it, not knowing exactly what I'm really seeing. I think I'm in shock because this can't be real. Suddenly, a giant fan, at least five feet wide, unfolds and my heart begins to palpitate. I move my eyes up the large fishtail and notice it's wrapped—or perhaps merges, with my rescuer's abdomen. I gape at the length of his long torso and chest before I notice something I didn't see before—slits open and close parallel on each side beneath his collarbone. *He has gills!*

I scream, but the man covers my mouth and he shakes his head wildly. I push him away as I scream even louder, trying to get up, but the weight of my backpack keeps me down—*of course*, Aunt Cora is inside!

My rescuer or whatever he is, grabs the back of my neck once more with one hand as he touches his forehead to mine and shakes his head gently while keeping his other hand over my mouth.

The motion of our foreheads rotating in contact with our noses barely touching and his hand between our mouths silences me. He keeps his brow to mine for a few minutes before backing away. I pull his hand from my mouth, though I'm scared to touch him. He doesn't take his eyes off me as he tries to pet me again, this time at the top of my head.

I duck away, avoiding his caress, and try to sit up, but my backpack still weighs me down. I scramble to untie the knot and I feel like I'm working on it for way too long when my rescuer's fingers reach over my waist and yanks, ripping the straps apart, and freeing me.

I swallow hard as I glance over to the fishtail then back to the hand, then back to the tail, then to the man's face, then back to the hand again resting at my waist.

Damn you, Aunt Cora!

Reluctantly, I look back at the man's strong but pitiful

face that is just staring at me with those blue eyes, like he's waiting for me to say or do something, but *he* hasn't said anything yet. He's just been *caressing* or *rubbing* or *patting* me like he's doing right now with his hand at my waist.

"You can't speak, can you?" I ask as I roll my whole body toward him.

He shakes his head. *No.*

"And you saved me?"

He smiles and nods. *Yes.*

Damn it. Either I'm dead, turned looney like my mother, or a fool for not believing my aunt.

I examine him more closely with my eyes. He doesn't seem to mind that I'm assessing more of his physical details, particularly his muscles. I'm sure it was easy for him to pull me out of the water. His body is completely absent of fat. Even his face boasts strength and masculinity.

His tail flicks against the sand and I glance over to see it move side-to-side across the sand as the sides of my mouth turn upside down and I gulp. He grabs my chin to face him and cocks his head like he's disappointed.

"I know!" I shout. "I get it! You're a mermaid or mer*man* or—"

I glance over to where his man parts might be, but I don't see anything except what looks like a flap over a bump or something. I try not to stare too hard before blurting out, "Or mer-*person*." I want him to know how grateful I am for saving my life, so I try to sound sincere, although I'm sure I sound crazy and not as the most appreciative person in the world when I say, "Thank you."

He grins halfheartedly.

Planting his hands at his sides and using his arms, he lifts his lower half and scoots himself closer to the water. I think he's leaving and for some reason. I feel sicker than I did earlier.

"No, wait!" I cry, and he turns to me but I don't know what to say. My mind is at odds with what's happening, yet I don't want him to go. "Is there any way I can repay you?"

He squints. His interest is piqued, but he doesn't move, except for his tail. I gulp as his tail flicks once more. He huffs with my reaction, looking more disappointed than he did earlier and he shakes his head, scooting back to the water.

"Wait, please!" I bellow, and he stops to bow his head. "There must be something I can do for you, something I can give you. I'm sure I should reward you in some way. You saved my life and, I'm sorry, but this whole thing is just taking me a minute to get used to. Is there anything I can get you? Anything you need?"

He looks enticed, his eyes widening along with his grin as he scoots back up to me.

"You *do* need something?" I ask genuinely excited. "Whatever it is, I'll try to get it for you."

I wish I had not spoken so eagerly. He gets close—*too* close, rolling his body right up to mine. I swallow hard. I'm not sure what I committed myself to, but he hesitates. He can't speak, so maybe he just doesn't know how to tell me.

"What is it?" I ask softly.

His eyes move down across my body like he's studying me. I hope to God he isn't about to eat me or something horrible like that, but then he reaches for the top of my shorts and tries to undo the button.

Panic shoots through me, and I grab his hand. "What are you doing?"

He looks me in the eye and we stare at each other for a minute before he wiggles his hand free of mine and tries to slip it under my shorts and underwear.

My face flushes as if it could get any hotter under this sun and I grab his hand again. "I don't understand."

He pulls his hand free of mine and we both notice my

hands are trembling, along with my teeth. I'm not cold--not with the hot sun blaring. I'm afraid. I don't know exactly what he's asking for, though I'm pretty sure it's something sexual.

He bows his head again and I see his gills open and close like he just sighed. He turns away from me back onto his butt or his rear or *whatever* and scoots towards the water.

"No, wait!" I yell.

He scurries faster like a seal, except he is more than twice the length of such an animal from head to tail.

I scamper to get up but trip, landing flat on my face as one of my boots slips off. I'm covered in sand and feeling foolish as tiny, solid grains of silicon stick to my eyes, nose, and mouth. I spit as I see him enter the water.

Catch him, Shelley! He's getting away!

I stand up and run into the still, azure water that slows me down, along with my one boot on one leg, which feels heavy again. The weight and the temperature of water—heavy and chilling—it shocks me, reminding me how I nearly drowned earlier. I halt, waist deep in the bay.

"Come back!" I call out, but there is no sign of him. "I'm sorry," I shout again and there's a part of me that desperately doesn't want to lose him. "I can give you what you want," I plead as I make a splash with my hands in hopes of getting his attention. "If you need what I think you're asking for, I'm happy to pay you your reward. Please, come back!"

The top of his head pops up out of the water right in front of me and I jolt in fear, falling back and crashing into the water, which fills every one of my senses. It's another reminder of my near-death experience and I panic once more, needing air.

Luckily, the water is shallow and I'm thankful it's easy to collect my feet under me. Digging my soles and my toes into the sand, I poke my head up above the water and wipe my face to get a good look.

He's still there—watching me, as his eyes glimmer from just above the water. His eyes are stunning, like sapphires, and his peachy bronze cheekbones are certainly sexy.

I reach out to touch the beautiful creature before me, my hand is wobbly. "I think I understand what you need," I say.

Droplets of bay water slip from his hair, over his cheeks, and down to his mouth as he brings his chin above the surface. He stares at me through my wobbling fingers and he brings his lips to my touch. He allows his soft, pink lips to glide across my fingertips and my heart races. His lips are at least worthy of a kiss, except I know he wants, or *needs,* much more.

"You want me," I whisper as I inch my body closer.

He nods.

"You want to make love to me?"

He smiles as if relieved and nods again.

"Will it hurt? Can you hurt me?" I ask.

His eyes squint and he looks confused but then, he chuckles and shakes his head. *No.*

"Okay," I say and take a big breath. "You can take—"

Before I can finish, his mouth presses hard on mine. I let him kiss me with lips that are as chilled as the water, yet soft like a rosebud. He tastes as human as any man I have ever kissed, except with a hint of salt.

His hand slips under my arm and wraps around my back as his other hand grips my hair from the back of my head. My legs begin to float as we move backward. My back meets the sand on the beach and he lays me down with my legs still in the water. Hovering over me, he stares into my eyes as I feel a tug at my waist—he hastily unsnaps the button to my shorts.

I hear splashing and tilt my head up to see him scooting

back as the fan of his tail is smacking at the water while he maneuvers himself. He yanks at my drenched shorts and underwear, which are putting up a fight as they stick to my skin, and he finally slips them down my legs passed one naked foot and then over the other still tied with a boot.

Gliding back on top of me, I feel his abdomen and skin rub with mine, but the rest of him is wedged between my legs—it's heavy, scaly, and awkwardly slippery like a fish. The vast end of a fish is between my legs and I have no idea how the rest of this is going to work, but I'm hoping *he* does.

He pulls up one side of my soaked shirt and pulls up my bra, wasting no time in wrapping his lips around my nipple to suckle and I gasp.

He knows exactly what he's doing.

I close my eyes and lie still, not sure what to think or do. I consider that maybe I *did die* and I'm in some type of Heaven or Hell or worse—Purgatory!

Although, it certainly feels a lot more like Heaven as his hand slides under the other side of my bra to massage my other breast while he keeps sucking.

Abruptly, he stops. I open my eyes and he's looking at me funny. "What's the matter?"

He reaches for my hand and puts it on his face, so I'm cupping his cheek and he slides his cheek back and forth over the inside of my palm.

"You want more than just to make love to me, don't you?" I ask, and he nods. I remove my shirt and bra, bringing my face up to his and lick his salty lips. "You want me to make love back to you. That's the reward you want—you need love."

His tail makes a big splash and I feel like it's raining. I can't believe what I'm about to do, but I'm sure Aunt Cora, and even Kumiko, would be proud.

I lean up to kiss him, wrapping my arms under his biceps

and digging my hands into the part of him that is human—mostly. He kisses me hard, fisting my hair and pulling me to rest flat on the sand.

Nuzzling my neck, he shifts his weight a little to one side. I feel his hand reach between my legs and a finger enters me, making me wetter than a jellyfish. He pulls his finger out quickly and I feel him doing something with his hands to himself down there. I try to tilt my head up to see, but he fists my hair tighter, so I can't look as he centers himself back over me.

Then, I feel it.

His erection, or whatever it is, at the center of my crease. My breath hitches as he glides into me. I close my eyes again to avoid the bright glare of the sun as he pushes himself further and further in—it's so damn deep! He thrusts himself in and out a few times and it feels like he's getting deeper.

"Ah!" I sigh, and he kisses me, burrowing his tongue into my mouth. I dig my claws deeper into his back, which makes him thrust harder.

Water droplets sprinkle my face as I escape his kiss to peer over his shoulders at his tail still making a splash.

It's crazy, but it turns me on. I feel like a goddess being showered by the spray of the ocean.

I wrap one leg around his fishtail and he lets out a soft, airy moan. He yanks at my hair tightly as he grunts and his whole body—torso and fishtail, jerk in wild motions within my grasp. His face looks like he is in ecstasy as he grunts deeply and comes in me, flooding me with his semen.

His body relaxes as he pulls himself out, but I don't want to let him go. He takes my hands from behind his back and lifts my leg to free himself of me. My heart sinks. I think he's done—that's all he wanted.

I want to cry. Moments ago, I was screaming at the sight

of him and now I'm about to weep because I'm about to lose him.

He sees my distress and kisses the insides of my palms, the ones Aunt Cora once read prophesying my death and rebirth several times over and which she said would make me a believer.

And I *do* believe her—I believe everything she ever said about merpeople and their stories, energies, bodies, and connectedness. I just wish I'd paid more attention, so I'd know how to stay connected like I need to right now.

He scurries back, exposing my naked body, and it makes me angry.

"So, that's it?" I shout. He looks at me, perplexed. "You rescue me, have sex with me, and leave? I should've known. Fin or no fin, you're still just a man," I sob. "I get it. Catch and release—there's plenty of fish in the sea." I smack the shallow water, stirring up the sand, causing a few grains to stick in my eye and I cry harder. "Oh my God!" I snap at myself. "What the hell am I even saying?"

I feel the water rise and fall over my waist, displaced by his weight and strength, as he swims back between my legs and kisses me. He kisses me so hard, my body ignites once more like I'm on fire despite the cool water. I swear I can feel steam rising from between us.

But then he just stops. His eyes wander to search for what lies behind me like he's been alerted to something. Grasping the coin hanging around his neck, he slips it off and places it over my head with a quick peck on the cheek. He points to his chest where his heart should be then points to the coin hanging above my heart. He kisses my lips once more and backs away, leaving me hungry for more.

I look down and take the coin in my hand to look at it. I'm sure it has some special meaning and I guess I should be thrilled he's given it to me, but the next thing I know, he's half underwater, diving in and disappearing.

I hear sirens behind me and I reach for my clothes, struggling to put them on.

Motherfuckers! Someone is invading my one psychic, cosmic, connected moment and I swear if my merman gets away they are never going to hear the end of my fire-breathing wrath.

"Wait!" I yell, going after my merman. I figure maybe I can swim out to him, but I trip on my other boot, this time landing a lot harder than I did before. My head knocks on what feels like a rock. My forehead stings. Reaching up to my head with my fingertips, I feel something wet and slimy —*blood*.

Men shout, coming up from behind me and I still wish to get away, to swim after my merman, but my body feels heavy like I'm drowning again, except I can't seem to fight to keep my eyes open or stay afloat.

3

BLUE

"What do you mean he can't talk?" The man in a long sleeve gray shirt and dark gray pants sounds angry.

I wouldn't argue with the doctor like that.

"He can't talk," says the short, bald-headed doctor with a long white coat that nearly touches the floor, "because his vocal chords do not work. The X-rays show he's suffered some type of trauma. From the look of things, it appears he has some scar tissue, likely from strong heat and smoke inhalation. He had to have been in a fire some years ago."

"Look, Doc. This guy shows up on the beach—naked and without I.D. I need to question him and you're saying he's mute?"

"And illiterate."

"You mean he can't read? So, he's deaf *and* dumb?"

"No, Sheriff," the doctor says. "He's not deaf or dumb. He can hear everything you're saying, and he clearly understands English. But he has no speech and, for now, he won't be able to answer your questions beyond a simple yes or no."

"How do you know he's not lying?" asks the man, who I understand is the sheriff.

"I don't," says Doc, "but I've never seen a case like this and I understand all the suspicion. He's behaved pleasantly, and a social worker is coming to see if she can help."

"So, is there anything else I should know?" asks the sheriff.

"I don't think he can walk."

I panic at the words Doc has spoken and I rip the white covers off my lower half. Despite what Doc says, I'm ecstatic and ready to do somersaults because they're there. *Legs!*

I attempt to lift a leg, but it doesn't move, so I try to wiggle a toe and it certainly moves—not that much, but it's moving.

I hear the doc go on. "His legs have some atrophy."

"What the hell does *that* mean? Astro—pee," asks the sheriff. "Don't tell me he pees himself too."

"Atrophy," corrects Doc. "It means he hasn't used his legs for some time and the muscle has degenerated to an extremely weak state. The CT scan shows with a little vitamin and protein supplementation plus physical therapy, he might be able to walk in a few months."

I don't understand everything Doc is saying, but I think he's saying my legs might not work right away, which they do look weak and feel weak to me. I try to wiggle my toe on my other foot and I smack the bed railing out of joy as I see my toe move.

"Well, someone's happy," says a familiar voice. It's Yanka. She works with Doc. There are several humans dressed like Yanka in this place, which I've figured out is a place of healing. Many of the humans, especially the women, come to look at me, but not so much to see me as a spectacle for doctoral study. They come and look at me as if I am something exotic, like a bird in a cage.

The women are all pretty. Every. Single. One. It's been too long since I've been this close to them, but Yanka really stands out from the rest. She keeps her long, pale blonde hair tied back, which exaggerates her features and wildly painted face. Her blue eyes, similar in color to mine, really stand out.

Yanka is nice, but she keeps shoving dry pellets in my mouth and uses a peculiar machine to blow air into what looks like a flotation device around my arm. She says it's to check my blood, but I don't see blood when the device blows up. I only feel like she's about to *stop* my arm from having any blood flow.

"Why did you take your covers off?" asks Yanka and I smile and point to my toes. She looks down at them as I just barely wiggle the big one. "Yay!" she rejoices and claps her hands. "That's great!" she says, but she pushes me back down and pulls up the covers.

"Listen, Blue," whispers Yanka as she traps my eyes with a stern stare as well as my arms with a firm tuck of the sheet around me. "The sheriff is coming in here to question you. I don't want you to worry though because I already made arrangements for you to come home with me."

I shake my head. I can't go home with Yanka. I have to look for my girl—my girl with earth green eyes who spits fire when she speaks. I'm sure as soon as she sees me she'll want me to go home with *her*.

"Don't shake your head at me," scolds Yanka. "If you can't find a place to stay, the sheriff's going to put you in the county jail."

County? I have no idea which county I'm in, but *jail?* That's a term I know far too well. I should have figured there'd be one around here somewhere.

"You don't want to go to jail, do you?" Yanka asks and I shake my head. "Great! So, you're coming home with me." Yanka smiles and reaches under the covers, sticking her hand between my legs to roll the two sacks of my *bawbels* between her fingers before grabbing at my shaft—my *Man Thomas,* which quickly stands at attention. "Doc says your cock probably works pretty good, so I'm sure *that's* good news," she smiles.

I look out to the doctor in the hall because the feeling of Yanka's hand at my crotch feels good yet makes me uncomfortable knowing someone else might walk in. I cough to alert her to remove her hand because the doctor and the sheriff are about to enter the room.

"What's your name, stranger?" the sheriff questions as he pushes his way in through the door.

"He can't speak, Pike," replies Yanka, who covers my standing Man Thomas with a pillow.

The sheriff, whose name I figure must be Pike, pushes Yanka to the side. A clap of thunder resounds, but it doesn't faze the sheriff a bit as he leans over my bed trying to intimidate me. If the sheriff knew my history and what I'm capable of, he might not be so eager to look down on me.

"The man looks to be in his late twenties, maybe thirty. I'm sure he didn't get through over two decades of life without some form of communication. Isn't that right stranger?" asks the sheriff, but I say nothing. "Where are you from?" he asks me. "And what's your name? Why don't you have any ID or personal effects on you?"

I remain still and silent. If they knew the truth, they wouldn't believe it. After hundreds of years, *I* still can't believe it. But here I am and I'm not going to make a peep or perform any action to draw attention to myself. I'm not going to blow this. As much as I want to get up and use my legs to walk—no, *run*—I'm going to force myself to sit and wait for the right moment to look for the girl from the bay.

"You look like you're thinking pretty hard," the sheriff comments as I mistakenly make eye contact with him.

The sheriff appears to be about the same age as Yanka—early thirties, except he certainly has more stress lines on his brow and around his eyes. His dark brown, nearly black eyes are recognizable and I search his face for more familiarity. I've seen him. I've seen him patrolling beaches before.

"There. You see?" The sheriff looks at the doc and then points to me. "This man is up to no good. He's up to something. I can see it in his eyes."

I look away.

The sheriff laughs. "I knew it! There's practically smoke coming out of this stranger's ears and I can hear all those gears grinding in that grisly skull of his."

I feel the sheriff lean in closer to speak in my ear. It's the same tactic slave traders used to irritate slaves for fun. I feel unfortunate to know a lot about the slave trade.

The sheriff continues to tease me, tempting me to push or hit him, which would give him an excuse to use his authority to whip me or lock me up. "Whatever you're planning, stranger," says the sheriff pointing his finger at my forehead, "I'm going to get to it before you will."

"All right, that's enough," Yanka protests. "Stop intimidating my patient before I call the orderlies on you, Pike."

Sheriff Pike gives me one more glance over with a wicked eye and a snicker and steps back as Doc comes up.

"Are you comfortable, Mr. Doe?"

I don't know why the people here keep calling me that—John Doe, but it works. Yanka prefers Blue, which I'm comfortable with, too.

I nod to Doc. Apart from the poking and prodding, I'm exceptionally comfortable. I'm surprised they would give a stranger such a comfortably firm bed. Whatever feathers they stuff them with must have come from at least a few hundred birds.

Doc continues, "I've ordered a high-protein diet plus

some physical therapy and the social worker will also be in to see you. I'm waiting on a call from the psychologist, maybe she can help you remember a few things."

"So, we can send your ass back to wherever it is you came from," interrupts Sheriff Pike, who points his finger at me again. "Don't get too comfortable, stranger. As soon as I get to the bottom of this, I'm shipping your ass outta my town."

Ship. It's been a couple of hundred years since I've been on one. I watched them from under the water. They've changed so drastically, from winded sails to giant metal buckets and heavy underwater tin cans. Over centuries, they keep getting bigger, becoming more of an eyesore than a vessel meant to travel, explore, and enjoy the seas.

I miss the boats of the old days—finely crafted wooden ships made by hand. There were boats as beautiful as the women who hand-sewed the outsized sails affixed to high masts making it easy for men atop of wooden decks to be blown across oceans.

But I've decided no more boats for me *or* fish *or* sand *or* endless salty seas. I want what all these humans have—to live on land.

I tug at the sheet Yanka tucked snug up to my shoulders as she, along with Doc and the sheriff, exit my room. Once they are out of sight, I pull at the sheet to expose my lower half and there they are again—*my own legs!*

But now, I want pants. I don't understand why they put me in a dress, not to mention it's backward and shows my arse. For heaven's sake, I'm sure there are some extra clothes lying around somewhere. This is a place of healing. In the days before I was cursed to reside in the sea, places of healing were primarily a place of death. Surely, there are pants lying around from some dead guy here somewhere. And shoes! I especially want to try the white ones with unusually bright colors that everyone is wearing that seems to make people bounce.

I might be getting ahead of myself. Doc says I can't walk yet, so I think I'd better see if he's right. In my day, physicians were sometimes madmen in disguise.

I yank at the contraption that traps me in the bed— bedrails, as Yanka called them, are intended to keep me from falling out, but I know she puts them up to keep me trapped so I'm stuck to take her prodding and pellets.

I yank at the bedrails again, but they won't budge. I figure I'm going to have to climb over. Turning and pushing myself up on the bed rails, I recognize my legs are, indeed, weak and I can hardly use them to help me. Leaning over the rails, I reach to the floor and feel a tight pull on my leg. The pain is excruciating as my thigh gets stuck.

I wiggle my waist and hear a familiar voice. It's *her* voice —the girl I've come for.

I push with all my might. Having legs again is not as easy as having fins, if I'm honest with myself, but I push harder. I gasp as my knee comes to a crash on the smooth hard floor. This is one of the rare times I'm glad I can't make a sound. I would've screamed at the sharp pain of my bone hitting the ground and probably whined, too, from the throbbing ache. But I have to get over this fall and be glad that no one heard the commotion I've made.

I look towards the door. I need to get to her before she's gone. I can hear her still talking, but she's not alone. She's talking to the sheriff. I listen intently.

"So, you don't remember anything?" he asks her.

"Nothing," she says.

"Shelley, I need you to be honest with me because the doc says your body shows evidence of nearly drowning and it's possible you might have been sexually assaulted. Did someone force themselves upon you?"

"I don't think so, but I really have no idea," she replies.

Shelley. Her name is Shelley and I wish the sheriff would quit interrogating her.

"The only reason we came out that way," he says, "is because a friend of yours called and said you were hiking up to Lovers Peak at which time she claims you reported a man was following you and you were scared and then your phone cut out."

"I don't remember that," says Shelley.

"What's the last thing you do remember?" asks the sheriff and I hear them stop in the hall.

"Honestly," she says, "I don't even know how I got to town. It must've been by plane. What day is it?"

I panic. *Is she serious? Does she really not remember our meeting or is she covering for me?*

I can see the pair of them now coming closer to the door and I use my elbows to scoot my body forward dragging my legs behind me. I get to the wall and try to pull myself up on a chair, but I can't get myself up there. I want her to see me, but I notice her bottom half rests in a chair with wheels, inching its way in view through the door. The sheriff's shoes I see are right next to her.

I crouch because I don't want the sheriff to see me. Pulling myself to the side of the chair in my room, I grab my legs, yanking them close to the wall to hide them so I can listen again as they speak at my door.

Shelley describes what she remembers up until a few days ago and it sounds genuine—she's lost her memory. She doesn't remember the small communications box she dropped into the water and the sheriff says he cannot recover it. It makes me ill to hear her mention she wants to leave town and go back to her home, wherever that is. It also sounds like she's been injured, but I did not leave her that way. She says Doc is planning to let her out of this place, a "hospital," tomorrow, but she's afraid of returning to her vacant aunt's home alone.

I need to speak to her. I need to help her remember.

I look at my legs—they're useless and only half healed. I rub my head, which is aching just as bad as my knee.

"You're welcome to stay at my place," the sheriff says.

I could stab him. I really could, but then I'll get thrown in jail. I toss the thought of killing the lawman out of my mind. Peeking around the chair, I see the sheriff's back is towards me as he tries to convince her to stay with him. I push myself out a bit further to see if I can get a better look.

Shelley looks beautiful, but she looks like she's been injured. She has bandages on her forehead. My heart aches for her. It's strange, but she has the same dress on that I do and my arse feels cold.

I see her wrap her hand around the coin hanging from her neck. I'm elated she still has it. *This is why I still have legs.* But the curse isn't broken yet, which why they won't work— she has to *love* me. I'm going to have to make her remember.

"Did you give this to me?" she asks the sheriff and it's evident she surely doesn't remember anything that's happened between us.

Sometime between the period I dove in the water to hide from the lawmen as they rolled up on the beach inside of their metal bucket carriages and when I surfaced to see them carrying her away, Shelley must've been injured and lost her memory.

"No," says the sheriff, "you had that on when I found you."

"But you did save me?" she asks.

The sheriff hesitates. He shifts back and forth as if he's contemplating what his answer should be, which had better. Be. The. Truth.

"Yes, I did save you," he says proudly.

Fucking bootlicker! I roll onto my side and slide myself

towards the door using my arms and hands to pull me as fast and as hard as I can go. I'm dragging myself across the hard, cold floor and my cheeks flush when I make eye contact with her.

"Oh my God!" Shelley yells. "What is that man doing?"

I grab onto the wheels of her chair and Shelley starts yelling. I try to speak to her. I try to motion to her with my hands pointing between the two of us so maybe she'll remember as the sheriff is yelling at me to "Back the fuck off." I feel my face hit the cold floor as the sheriff gets on top of me. He pulls at my arms and shackles them behind my back.

I look up to Shelley who looks terrorized. I thought if she saw me, she'd remember.

Doc arrives and starts arguing with the sheriff to keep me in the hospital, but I believe the sheriff is going to win this argument as he starts to drag my bare arse across the shiny slick floor. Yanka has come to my aid, as well, but I already know she's not going to be able to persuade the sheriff to put me back in the bed. I'm confident the sheriff is taking me to jail just as he wanted from the start. I look Shelley in the eyes as she gets farther away and I look at her hand on the coin.

"No wait!" she calls out and the sheriff pauses, turning to her.

Shelley dangles the coin. She's curious, tilting her head to one side to look at me. "Is this what you were after?"

I take a big breath. My human lungs feel so dry in this building. I nod. The coin is no longer mine anymore because I gave it to her, but I nod, *yes*, with exaggeration in hopes she will be able to connect the coin back to me—to us.

I know she loves me even if it's just a little because my fin is gone and I have legs. If I can get her to love me a little bit more, then maybe the curse will end. I'll no longer be a spear on Poseidon's trident and I'll be human and walking again.

4

SHELLEY

*P*ushing the wheels on my wheelchair to bring me closer to my hospital room door, I can hear the social worker finishing her interview with the stranger.

Pike tried to take the stranger off in handcuffs, but Dr. Subler fought with Pike about it. I agree.. the stranger clearly needs help.

I'm not exactly sure what the strange man was trying to do when he grabbed my chair. I found out later when Pike reluctantly put the stranger back in his room that the poor guy can't speak, he's illiterate, and he can't walk. I do feel sorry for him. He's clearly been through a lot and I can tell the social worker thinks so, too. I already heard her ask him several times if he'd been locked up against his will.

"It's a very strange case," the social worker says as she speaks in the hallway with the doctor and the sheriff. I move my ear close to the door so I can listen without being seen.

"Where's he from?" asks Pike. "And when's he leaving?"

"He says he's from here, from Porterman's Bluff."

"Doc, I thought you said he can't speak," replies Pike.

"He can't speak," says the social worker. "And you were

right, doctor. I suspect he's illiterate, but he communicates well with pictures and maps."

I hear the doctor. "Pictures? What else did you find out?"

"I think he's a fisherman or sailor of some type. I was able to narrow most of the focus of his knowledge on things related to marine life and oceanography, but when I spoke about social services and simple things like cell phones or anything related to technology, he clearly doesn't understand a thing."

"Were you at least able to get an address and pinpoint exactly where he lives?" asks Pike.

I hear the social worker chuckle. "He says he lives at the Peak. When I showed him a map, he pointed right to it."

"Lovers Peak?" Pike asks sounding as surprised as I feel. "That's along the edge of Cora Morae's property."

"Which now belongs to Shelley," adds the doctor, "and could explain why he might want to talk to her. I suspect he's homeless and perhaps he's been living out there, although it still doesn't make any sense how he's been able to take care of himself in his condition."

"I don't know either," says the social worker, "but I've given him every resource available to him. He has several business cards and brochures on where to get help. It's shameful he can't read all of it, but perhaps someone here can help him if he's going to be here for a few days."

"The hospital has no reason to keep him," replies Dr. Subler. "I hate to turn him back out on the street, but I don't have a choice."

"He can always sleep in one of my open cells," Pike blurts out.

"C'mon, Sheriff," says the social worker rather sassily.

"Well, honestly, I can't hold him either," Pike replies. "Unless Shelley wants me to lock him up for attacking her earlier, he hasn't committed any crimes."

I think about what happened when the stranger grabbed the wheels to my wheelchair and look down at the coin hanging around my neck. I don't know where the coin came from or how I got it. It's heavy, like solid gold. It shines luminously even under the hospital's fluorescent lights. A single link is welded to the edge where it hangs from a golden chain and it has the portrait of a woman on it—or perhaps it's a man with a wig, but the whole thing looks ancient. Maybe it's his—the stranger's. Maybe he wants it back.

Multiple footsteps head down the hall and I'm thankful the social worker, Dr. Subler, and Pike are leaving. I roll my chair into the doorway and look down the hall—it's clear. I roll myself down to the next doorway almost banging into the wall. *I hate this stupid chair.*

Dr. Subler says I must stay seated at all times so I don't fall down because of the "unpredictability" of my concussion, so I stay seated as I reverse and roll into the stranger's doorway.

The stranger is lying in his bed with one hand over his face like he's in distress or in pain. I notice all the paperwork the social worker mentioned she gave him is sprawled across the floor.

I roll myself in and watch him reach the top of his thighs with both hands and start to massage them.

"Does it hurt?" I ask.

He jerks his head at me. He's cute, in a rugged way, with his black hair kinked at the ends in some places like it needs to be washed and conditioned. He's also very tan, so it wouldn't surprise me if he *is* homeless living on the beach at the bay.

He doesn't say anything. He just sort of gawks at me and I'm glad his legs don't work or he might try to attack me again.

"Do your legs hurt?" I ask again, slower and little louder.

He nods and sticks his hand through the bed rails like he's reaching for me. It makes me nervous when he waves at me to come over. I debate whether I should turn my chair around or just get up and run out, but then I remember the coin. I lift it to dangle as I did earlier. "Do you know anything about this?" I ask. "Have you seen it before?"

He smiles and sits up, leaning in my direction. He's clearly excited and points to himself.

"You think this is yours?" I ask and he nods.

Why am I not surprised? I think he wants it, but I don't want to let it go. It's all I have of my memory for the last few days, so I grip the coin in my palm.

"How did I get it?" I ask.

He points to himself and then back at me.

"Are you saying you gave this to me?"

He nods with so much excitement, the longer tendrils of his hair fall over his face so he pushes them back with his fingers, exposing his gorgeous blue eyes.

"I don't believe you," I say and his face kinks, stunned. His eyes widen to a brighter blue, blaring with desperation—a desperation that says he's probably homeless. "I think you're lying."

I watch him fall back to the bed and cover his face with his palms again. Now I feel dismayed. I didn't mean to come in here to upset him. I'm sure he's been through enough as both the social worker and the doctor stated.

"I'm sorry, I shouldn't have bothered you."

He sits up and reaches for me. He's shaking his head wildly and it looks like he's trying to get out of the bed. He starts to push himself over the rail and I'm pretty sure he's going to fall over.

I get out of the wheelchair and run to push him back in the bed before he falls off and breaks his arms. He already can't walk and I'm not going to be responsible for injuring him more. I try to hurl him back flat, but he grabs my hand, leaning forward, to kiss my fingers.

"Stop it!" I say and try to push him back again. "Get in the bed before you fall over."

I notice he's not going after the coin at all but instead, reaches for my face with his lips so I smack him.

He stops moving as we are both shocked I did that. My hand hurts a lot more than it should like it's been ripped open. I look in my palm and see scratches and dried blood as if I struggled in some way. For whatever reason, I have a feeling the stranger knows about my wounds. I show him my palm.

"Do you know how I got these?"

He looks into my eyes then points to me and I follow his finger as he points in the air above his head. He makes a zigzag motion and from what he's doing, I figure I'm his finger and it looks like I'm falling. But then he stops and moves his finger quickly up into the air, like I'm flying, and then drops it to his lap. He points to himself and then to me before reaching both hands between his lap and raises them like he's lifting something, lifting me.

"I don't understand," I tell him. "Are you saying I fell?"

He nods.

"So, what is this?" I ask, pointing in his lap.

He makes a bunch of other motions with his hands, but I don't get it and it frustrates me.

"Tell me how I got the coin," I demand.

He looks me in the eyes again and points to his chest and then back at the coin that hangs from my neck. He insists he gave it to me, but I don't understand how a homeless man could possess such a thing. It could explain his eagerness to communicate. I don't really need the coin as much as he probably does. I suspect it has some monetary value, which could buy him some clothes at least.

I decide to give it back, but as I grip the chain around my neck and start to pull it over my head he stops me. He shakes his head wildly again and grabs my hands gently, helping me wrap my fingers around the coin and pushing it against the top of my breast.

"Don't you want it back?" I ask.

He shakes his head and pats his fingers over my hand that holds the coin over my chest.

"You want me to keep it?"

He nods in confirmation.

"If you don't want it, I'll take it," says Yanka, the nurse. "And you're not supposed to be out of that chair, Shelley," she scolds.

Yanka comes up behind us, dressed in a tight white, low-cut V-neck T-shirt that exposes her nipples as they poke through her non-padded bra atop huge melon-sized breasts. Her denim miniskirt hugs the bottom of her ass and her four-inch high platform wooden sandals make her legs look as long as a giraffe's.

She places a small pile of folded clothing onto the end of the bed and I notice the stranger is now staring at her with a ridiculous grin as he stares at Yanka's tits. I admit I'm getting jealous. But my jealousy turns into embarrassment as Yanka pushes me aside to reach under the bed rails and releases them. The stranger smiles at her as though she just set him free.

"Where's he going?" I ask.

Yanka turns her head to me as her body continues to lean over the stranger, keeping her ass in the air like she wants to make sure both the stranger and I know who has the power of authority as well as seduction. "Blue's coming home with me," she says.

"Blue?" I ask. "Is that his name?"

"Are you fucking blind?" Yanka asks me. "Do you *not* see

those gorgeous blue eyes of his? Blue is coming home with me where I can get him all cleaned up."

"But he's homeless. Aren't you afraid... of..." Both of them turn to me with a look of perplexity or perhaps annoyance and I gulp. "I just meant—"

"We *know* what you meant, Shelley. But, if there's anyone here who's likely to be a psycho, it's *you*. You come from a long line of psychos. Blue here wouldn't hurt a soul," smiles Yanka with a twinkle in her. "Would you, Blue?"

The stranger—or *Blue*, shakes his head as Yank strips off the top of his gown. His tan covers ripped muscles, which I couldn't see hiding underneath. Yanka puts a white V-neck T-shirt on him. I admit he already looks better—*hotter*, but I roll my eyes at the sight of their matching clothing.

Yanka is the town slut, but she also has a big heart. She doesn't just rescue people in the hospital. She rescues critters, too—dogs, cats, birds, raccoons, squirrels. It doesn't surprise me that she feels the need to rescue a homeless man.

I try to correct myself. "I meant that you just met the guy."

Yanka laughs haughtily. "What's he going to do, Shelley? Stalk me? Chase me around the house with a butcher knife? He can't walk and he still needs medical care."

I feel imprudent. I grip the coin Blue says he's given to me, wondering if I should hand it over to Yanka who deserves it much more than I do.

"Besides," Yanka continues, "sometimes you meet someone and you just know you're connected. You just know he deserves everything you can give him."

Yank winks at Blue, but he looks at me and I feel a pang in my bones.

Yanka notices the look Blue just gave me. "What are you doing in here anyway?" she snaps at me. "You need to get out and give this man some privacy."

"I'm sorry." I take a few steps back towards the doorway.

I watch the two of them together—Yanka helping him, with her big heart, to get him dressed in the bed as she smothers him with her big tits while he smiles, looking happy about it. It makes me uneasy and I suddenly feel like I'm drowning. I feel like I can't breathe—watching the two of them together. I think I'm crushing on Blue a little.

Gripping the coin firmly in my hand, I turn to walk away and I hear a cheer behind me. "Hurray!" Yanka boasts to Blue. "You just wiggled all your toes."

5

SHELLEY

*P*ike helps me get into the wheelchair and puts the plastic bag stuffed with my clothes, which are stained brown and stink like dead fish, plus my backpack and boots on top of my lap. He pushes me down the hall and we pass the room where I last saw the stranger, Blue, getting dressed with Yanka's help. The sheets are tucked tight to the mattress and I look down at the coin hanging around my neck.

"You should have that appraised," says Pike. "I bet its worth some money."

Pike's nice even though he comes across as being a tough guy. He's a few years older than me and by the time I was in high school, he was already a police officer. The last time I came to visit Aunt Cora with Kumiko two years ago he asked to take me to dinner. Kumiko called me a dummy when I declined. "Just the thought of handcuffs should've forced you to give a 'yes' at least for *one* night," Kumiko said.

But not getting involved with anyone from this town has and always will be my best policy. I was a virgin until I went to college, then I was a slut. I straddled over every set of two legs that came with a penis. After college, I calmed down, only sleeping with two men the year after, but I haven't had sex with anyone in the last year. At least I don't think I have. I can't recall the last week—Dr. Subler says I have amnesia, which makes me worry I might have slept with someone in town. The space between my legs does feel a bit raw like it's been used recently.

Pike parks the chair next to the passenger door of his police car and bends over to lock the wheels. I see him checking me out and I hate it. I don't hate that he's doing it, I just hate that I'm still in the hospital gowns—one wrapped in the front and the other wrapped around my back so my ass doesn't show. With my fair skin peeping out of the oversized gowns and the dark circles under my eyes clashing with my strawberry blonde hair, I'm sure I look like I'm dressed for Halloween as a freaky ghost.

Pike assists me to get into the car, even though I really don't need any help, so I fuss with him to let go. "You already saved me once," I tell him and he smiles.

"You don't sound so happy about it," he says as he shuts the door.

I feel ashamed. He *did* save my life. I should probably show him a little gratitude. I just hope he doesn't ask for any kind of reward...

Reward!

I pick up the coin and look at it. I think I did something to get this. maybe I earned it and it was my reward for some-thing. I think about the stranger—about Blue.

"You're staring at that thing pretty hard," says Pike as he gets in the driver's seat. "It makes me suspicious you know something about that stranger we picked up."

I grip the coin in my palm and tuck it under my gown. "Sheriff, honestly, if I knew anything, I'd tell you."

I'm sure I sounded annoyed as Pike changes his tone. "I'm

sorry, Shelley," he says. "I didn't mean to sound like I was interrogating you. It's my job and I don't know how to turn it off."

I feel guilty. *Again.* "Thank you for saving my life," I tell Pike.

"You don't have to thank me," he replies as we pull out of the hospital parking lot and head to Aunt Cora's. "That's part of my job, too."

"I feel like I should repay you in some way." *Whoa!* Hearing the words come out of my mouth feels like some serious déjà vu.

"You don't owe me anything," he says.

I look directly at him, noticing his face like it's the first time ever. Under his dark sunglasses, he looks older than he should, probably from the stress of his job. Not to mention, this is a coastal town, so I'm sure his face gets exposed to a lot of sun causing more wrinkles as he's out tracking criminals during the day. I bet he hardly gets enough gratitude for that kind of work.

"I *want* to repay you somehow," I insist. "You knew my Aunt Cora. She would insist I reciprocate the favor."

"You believe in all that psychic energy stuff?" Pike asks.

"I don't know," I say, "but it seems like a good policy to have—too reciprocate good deeds. She used to say it—"

"Keeps the universe positive," Pike interjects. "Oh yes, I knew your Aunt Cora very well along with all her aphorisms."

I let out a snicker, but it hurts to hear Pike talking about her. I hadn't talked to her much before she died.

"How about this?" starts Pike. "How about you go with me to the Pirate Fest tonight?"

"You mean the *Booty* festival?" I snark. "Where everyone shakes their booty?"

Pike laughs, but it's true. The annual Pirate Fest falls on

the Friday following the summer solstice. It reportedly started two or three hundred years ago as a celebration to honor the founder of our town, Averill Porterman, who was a captain in the British Navy a few hundred years ago. It wasn't until recent years that historians discovered some naughty truths about the Captain, and the festival has turned just as naughty. Sure, there's a parade and a bunch of kids' stuff for families like balloons and a petting zoo, but once the sun goes down, Main Street turns into a Booty festival. Students from the nearby university show up just after dark and boobs and beer litter the street as asses stuffed in short shorts jiggle to the pumping sounds of raunchy pop songs. The whole town is into it. It's the one night where it seems acceptable for everyone, young and old, to misbehave.

"You don't have to show your booty," jokes Pike.

"Won't you be working?" I ask.

"Yeah, but you can keep me company. Main Street will be packed, but believe it or not, it can get boring for the first few hours until the sun goes down. Then it gets crazy. I can have someone take you home at nightfall or you can hang out and shake your booty. It's up to you."

"I bet you'd like that, wouldn't you?" I ask as Pike pulls up to Aunt Cora's house along the shore.

"I would, actually. Yeah," he replies smiling as he throws the cop car into park in front of the beach house that looks more like a pool shack.

I can't help but smile as well while I check out his ass as he gets out of the car. I'm so fucking horny for some reason. I felt like this at the hospital, too. It's an unshakable yearning as if I want to be with someone. I finally feel like I want to connect with someone, almost the way Yanka and Blue seemed to instantly connect.

Pike opens my door and helps me out. Of course, I could be feeling like this because of the whole *hero* thing. Pike looks good in his uniform. *What girl doesn't like a man in blues?* Pike saved my life and I don't think it's unreasonable to want to fuck him...

But I do feel a little irritated. I wonder if Yanka is fucking Blue right now.

6

BLUE

*T*hese *damned fur bags won't stop yapping!*
"I don't know why they're behaving so poorly,"
Yanka states as she snips at another lock of my hair. "They usually settle down by now after they've met someone new."

She walks away, leaving me in the bathroom to quiet her pets, but they yap louder with more anger like they are trying to warn her about the unnatural creature she invited in to share their space. I'm getting tired of all this noise. It hurts my ears and I'm not used it. I'm used to the voices of whales as they sing their love songs to their lifelong mates.

The lights flicker as a flash of bright light pierces through the windows, which is followed by a *boom* that vibrates heavily through the skeleton of Yanka's wooden house.

"Oh no!" cries Yanka. "I hope it doesn't rain," she says and pauses to study her fur bags. The animals are quiet. "Well, that shut you all up, didn't it?"

I hear a few more whines from two of the four dogs and thunder cracks through the sky once more. The sound is so close it almost sounds as though it's ripping from one end of the ceiling to the other across Yanka's pink and white house.

It's enough to keep her nasty critters from making any another peep.

Yanka continues to cut my hair, pulling out a fat wand of some type that makes a lot of noise and I push her hand away. "I'm not going to hurt you with it," she insists. "I'm just going to use the clippers to trim the sides."

Taking a big breath, I watch her in the mirror. She puts the clippers to my head and, surprisingly, it feels good, but I'm not so sure about the loss of hair. I've never had hair this short, not even when we had an infestation of head lice aboard the Annabelle, my most favorite and last ship I sailed on. I wouldn't let the portly captain allow the butcher to cut my hair. I took a lashing for it, but the good captain grew fond of me after that—I stood my ground. Of course, we are brothers now and I've grown fond of him, too, but I'm glad I haven't seen him in a decade. I certainly don't want him to know I have legs just yet—he'd be jealous.

When Yanka appears to be finished, she looks in the mirror and drops the clippers. "Heaven help me," she says, grabbing her chest. "I cannot wait to take you to the festival tonight. I have never seen anyone as handsome as the likes of you."

My face flushes with embarrassment and I look at myself. Truthfully, I think I look like an officer of our Majesty's Royal Navy, like my brother, the Captain. His uniform always looked freshly pressed and his wig perfectly curled with fresh white powder, which made his gray eyes sparkle like diamonds. Spoiled rich brats in command are the only ones who could afford to look so...*clean*. That's how I look—clean.

I wish I could say the same for Yanka's home. It's ironic she works in the hospital where she was so sterile about everything—always washing her hands, sometimes wearing a mask, and folding tape and sheet corners so they were at perfect sharp angles.

But her home? There are way too many frilly things hanging from every corner of the house—on the doors, on the handles, over the magic box that provides entertainment. Humans seem to like their magic boxes, but it's hard to watch when Yanka's large kettledrum holders are blocking the view as she stands between me and the mirror finishing my cut. Plus, there are mountains of makeup spilled and sprawled over every countertop from the bathroom to her bedroom and I wonder if I should mention my suspicion of rouge as making women go mad from back in my day when I was a sailor.

I also can't get over the hair. There's hair everywhere—dog hair, cat hair, *Yanka's* hair.

Yanka rubs her hands through my new, shorter mane and her fingers feel good on my scalp, making my eyes close. As I feel the heat of her breath close to my face, I open my eyes and she tries to kiss me, but I put my head down to look at my legs, a reminder of why I'm here, so her lips smack against my forehead. I can tell Yanka is disappointed as she lets out a small, impassioned huff that warms my face.

"You have someone, don't you?" she asks.

I close my eyes. I don't want to say anything and I'm glad I can't.

"That's okay," she says coming behind me as she brushes the cut hair off my bare shoulders. although it's not the hands of the girl I came for, I enjoy Yanka's touch. She hugs me from behind and speaks in my ear. "I'm going to be so good to you," Yanka says, "that I'm going to make you forget all about where you came from and whoever it is that seems to have forgotten all about you." Yanka bends down to nibble on my ear, sending a blissful tingle through my chest, hips, and down to my legs until I am covered in goosebumps.

I've missed this—being with humans and being human. More than anything, I've missed the touch of a woman, especially from a sexy, beautiful woman, which Yanka is surely. And there is a small piece of me that wishes she could, indeed, make me forget the last nearly three hundred years.

7

SHELLEY

I hear a siren. It's Pike coming to pick me up. I check my face one more time in the mirror, gazing at the gash on my head held together by two small stitches. It hurts, along with the rest of my body. I have scratches on my knees, bruises on my bottom, and I can still see tiny bits of dirt embedded deep in the scrapes on my palms.

I turn my palms away. I'm tempted to read them to see if they can give me any clue as to what happened to me since I have no idea what happened.

I also wish I could call Kumiko. She knows a little bit about what led up to my amnesia. Plus, I owe her for saving my life by calling the sheriff, from halfway across the planet, to come look for me.

As I'm looking at my stitches again in the mirror, I see one of Aunt Cora's paintings in the reflection. She loved to paint. She painted the whole house, both inside and out, the same teal color of the sea when it's reaching over the sand on a bright sunny day. The painting, hanging by a fish hook with fishing line, is of me as a chubby child with rose-colored cheeks wearing a tiny red tube top and a tiny red skirt with a big cheesy smile as I hold a fish in my palms. *Catch of the Earth*, she entitled it. I don't know why she'd paint me playing with a blue-green fish, which has almond-shaped rather than round blue eyes that look almost human.

It makes me laugh. I never touched fish as a kid. I thought they were too slimy and she knew this. "Don't be cruel to creatures of the sea," she used to say, "even though they will be jealous of you. The sea will forever be jealous of the earth because it's the earth that holds the sea." Aunt Cora liked to speak in riddles. Sometimes, their meanings were clear as day, while at other times, I had no clue as to what she meant.

Pike sounds his siren again and I hustle out of Aunt Cora's beach house in my cross-back, short, coral halter dress that scoops low in the front. Pike comes out of his car to greet me and hands me a bouquet of long-stemmed, white, tiny, but tightly packed flowers.

"What's this?" I ask.

"I thought you might like them. Your Aunt liked them. I used to catch her picking them on the side of the road."

"You know they're weeds. Right, Pike?"

Pike tosses them down to the ground with the rest of the weeds growing in the dry, sandy soil of Aunt Cora's front lawn. "Shit! If I had known that, I swear I would've stopped at the florist. I just thought maybe you were the type who preferred *au natural.*"

I laugh as Pike opens the door for me. "So, what the hell would your aunt pick them for?" he asks.

"Her potions and lotions and stuff," I say as I get in the car. "People paid her a lot of money for that junk."

Pike peeks down at me. "If she put it in her love potions then maybe I should pick it back up and give it to you."

I laugh again. It's cute. I never saw Sheriff Pike so charming and I can't help but allow my eyes to wander over the small hints of skin allowed to show beyond his long-sleeved sheriff's uniform as we head to the Pirate Fest.

I know he's taking his time to get there because other officers keep calling him on the radio to ask him what's taking so long. I like the attention, but if he tries any harder in pursuing me, I'm going to have to tell him I have no plans to stay in this town and I'm sure it'll ruin the night for both of us.

When we get to the festival, it's just as I remember. Main Street is flooded with kids in pirate costumes carrying plastic swords as parents chase, scream, and wonder why they allowed their youngsters to arm themselves with pointed weapons. Dads wear fake beards with fake parrots on their shoulders while moms are dressed like sluts. It's the one night of the year where it's okay for every mother to be sexy and let her bosom and bottom hang out.

It smells like a carnival and Pike buys me a pretzel and a beer. It's sad he can't drink with me, but I feel comfortable knowing I *have* a designated driver instead of *being* the driver for a change.

After Pike buys me a second beer, I question whether he's trying to get me drunk so he can put some moves on me later, but I can tell he's starting to regret asking me to come as his date. As we walk through the street, his eyes and mind are so busy trying to keep up with everything going on he can hardly finish a sentence through our conversations.

After a couple of hours, and my fourth beer, Pike leads me to a tattoo stand and asks me to wait so he can check on some kids reported as missing. I don't mind he has to go. I like watching tattoos being made. I watched Kumiko get a dragon tattoo over her shoulder and down her arm like a sleeve. I didn't have the heart to tell Kumiko Aunt Cora thought it was a bad thing to do because she believed Kumiko cursed herself by putting a dragon on her arm. Of course, I don't believe any of that and I enjoy watching the level of detail that goes into a tattoo and the artist's commitment to the art of also inflicting pain on another human being. I enjoy watching patrons flinch, especially those that cry.

This is the tattoo artist's busiest night of the year. Half the town will wake up in the morning with a permanent symbol of regret and the later it gets into the night, the bigger the tattoo and regret will be.

I watch a woman tighten her face and squeeze her eyes shut as ink is stabbed a hundred times a minute into her soft flesh atop the upper portion of her breast. Her tattoo looks like the face of the man standing next to her. When I see him, I can't help but feel remorse for her. He's not bad looking, but he does have a Mohawk and the artist has decided to include the enormous fake clip-on hoop ring I assume is supposed to make the guy look like a pirate. Unfortunately for him, he doesn't look anything like a pirate and neither does the handsome guy sitting nearby.

My heart skips a beat as the guy sitting down looks familiar, but I don't know anyone that looks that good. He smiles with amusement as he watches the woman laying on her back, having her breasts tortured, squeals. His smile is as wide as the ocean and the idea floods my mind—the two of us. Together. On the beach. In the sand.

The thought is peculiar and I finish my fifth beer then toss it into a trashcan as I try to maneuver myself between the crowd to get a better look at the guy.

He's sitting in a wheelchair and I see a hand come up from behind him to tap him on the shoulder. As the woman is bending over to speak in his ear, his smile gets even bigger and he looks up to her, so she bends further to give him a quick peck on the cheek. She hands the handsome man a beer before she turns to watch the torture and she brushes her blonde hair away from her face. It's Yanka.

I feel sick. Blue is fucking hot with the short haircut Yanka gave him and the clothes she dressed him in—snug jeans and a trendy fitted light blue cotton shirt. I look down at the coin dangling around my neck and feel like a dumb ass. *I'm such a horrible person!* I don't know why—maybe because I'm drunk, but I want him. I want Blue.

I look back at them and this time he's looking at me. My body shivers as a breeze blows through the street and the crackling of thunder resounds above. My head tilts up towards the sky as flashes of light ripple through the clouds and the entire crowd of festival attendees gasp as thunder rolls through our skulls, hands, and to the center of our bones.

I look back at Blue, but unlike everyone else, he's not looking up—he's still watching me. I see him nudge the wheels of his chair as the crowd begins to thin.

Suddenly, a hand wraps around my elbow and Pike starts to pull me. "Let's go this way," he says as rain pours like a heavy shower out of nowhere.

I hesitate, but then Yanka pushes on Blue's chair handles so I follow Pike. People are screaming, holding their hands over their heads as they make their way towards any dry place they can find, which is nowhere.

Pike continues to yank on my arm and leads me to the old library at the center of Main Street. we walk into the century-old, thick, wooden doors. The book depository is well-lit and smells like mold. It's also chilly inside so I smooth my forearms with my hands to wipe the rain away and I feel myself sway. *I think I'm tipsy.*

"Hi, Sheriff," a redhead with ruby red glasses wearing a

long black and white floral skirt and conservative yellow top, says to Pike. She seems to be in her early thirties, too young to be dressed in ol' lady clothing. I wonder how I've never seen her before. "Hello, Shelley," she says to me and I'm annoyed.

"How do you know who I am? I don't know who *you* are?" I say, pointing in her face. I wouldn't normally do something like that, but I'm feeling brave. Must be the booze.

"Someone may have had too many beers," replies Pike as he puts my hand down for me.

"I'm Athena, the librarian and the City Council recently gave me the title of town historian. Sheriff Pike also employs me as well," she says too proudly for someone who I know wasn't born here and probably shouldn't have been entrusted with so much. Not to mention, her chin goes up too high when she speaks, like she's some kind of goddess among her pillars of books, but I know what she really is—*a nerd.*

I roll my eyes and Pike rubs the back of his head. *I'm horny but he's not gettin' any tonight.*

"Listen," he says to Athena, "can I leave Shelley with you? I know you're only supposed to be open as a designated shelter area for emergencies, but I need to get back out there to ensure some order."

Athena's lips open and quiver, "Uh...." is all she says as her tongue stumbles back and forth between her teeth. She's not remotely interested in being my babysitter until she catches a glimpse of my chest. "Where did you get that?"

"I'm guessing my mother," I say as I look down at my tits, which look awesome in this dress. It's funny to me she'd even ask, but Pike isn't laughing when he corrects me.

"She's talking about the coin, Shelley, so why don't you stay here and you two can talk about it and I'll be back in a little while."

Athena nods, so Pike leaves and I feel awkward. Athena reaches to my chest and grabs the coin. She flips it around between her fingers as she removes her glasses to get a closer look. *This woman does not understand boundaries!* I tilt my head back when, suddenly, I'm on my ass.

It hurts, but the feeling of falling felt good for some odd reason and an image of the bay floods my mind. It reminds me of my childhood as well as something peculiarly unfinished. It felt good to fall until I landed on the ground.

"Are you okay?" Athena asks as she helps me get to my feet. "Let's sit down."

She leads me to a big table between several bookshelves. I stumble a few times thanks to the buzz I have from one too many drinks. Athena helps me and it's plausible I may have been too hasty judging her, as she seems very sweet in helping me to sit down—until her voice sours.

"Where did you get that?" she asks and this time she's the one with her finger pointed at me. "Did your aunt give that to you? How long have you had it?"

"I don't know," I say gripping the coin between my fingers.

"What do you mean you don't know?" Athena barks. "*Who* gave it to you?"

I gulp. Blue says he gave it to me, but not exactly. He sort-of motioned he did. I'm also not so sure I should tell her because it's clear she's overly eager to get her hands on it. And I'm *not* letting it go since it's my only link to my missing memory.

Athena takes off her glasses and puts them on the table. "Look, Shelley," she sighs and I still don't know how she knows me. "I'm working on a doctorate degree. I'm a lover of history as well as mythology and folklore. I moved here two years ago to finish my research on some of the coastal sea lore. This town, Porterman's Bluff, and its surroundings are infested with sightings of mystical creatures and magic and history—"

I yawn, unable to listen to her babble as my head starts to throb. Athena huffs at me. "How attached are you to that thing on your neck?"

I quickly come to my senses and clutch the coin. "I'm very attached."

"Can I borrow it?" she asks trying to sound nice though it really sounds like she's whining.

"Not a chance."

She slams her hands down on the scratched up wooden table and stands up. I watch her stomp away and in a few minutes, she comes back dropping a stack of old books.

Oh, God. If I'd known I'd be looking at books instead of booties, I would've stayed home.

"Look at this," she says. Athena looks like a crazy person as she flips through the books. if there's anyone who knows what crazy looks like, it's me. Athena rolls her eyes at me when she catches me yawning again. I don't mean to be rude, but I can't help it. She finally picks a book and slides it over to me. "There. See?" she asks, indicating something.

I glance over to where her finger is pointed. I'm not sure if I'm supposed to be excited, but all I see is a picture of a coin, which matches mine, among other images of coins categorized under a date labeled 1727 to 1760.

"So, what?" I ask, still swaying in my seat as the oversize hall of books spins about me.

She huffs and rolls her eyes again then pulls another much smaller book covered in fitted plastic, which I'm sure is intended to preserve it. Athena opens the book, which looks like a journal consisting of scribblings and drawings that are very good, but they are mostly depictions of naked women doing naughty things. It's clear the women are not

from this time. their features are drawn with more volup-
tuousness than images of this day and age. They also have
hair on their privates—lots and lots of curly, thick hair. As
the pages advance, the drawings become better and include
greater detail. Athena flips through the book and I'm semi-
amused by the evidence of porn dating back a few centuries
until there is an image of a ship.

"Stop," I say. Aboard the ship are men doing random tasks
—cleaning, fishing, and on the lookout. Many have long hair
and beards though a few wear wigs like the officers of America's revolutionaries. They look as familiar to me as Aunt
Cora's paintings and books back at her beach house. Staring
at a few of the long-haired men, my skin prickles as one of
the mates looks familiar. He's almost recognizable and an
eerie feeling washes over me as the room stops spinning.

I notice Athena's tiny grin with my intrigue. She turns the
page to a drawing of two ships. one is drawn on fire. Flames
rise from the belly of the ship, which shows a darkened
woman, a slave, drawn naked and in chains in the center of
the vessel. I don't understand it completely since it depicts
pre-revolutionary naval officers and crew atop one ship
watching the fiery destruction of the other.

I sigh. Athena turns the page once more and the same
slave woman is sitting on a wave holding what looks like a
pitchfork. I lean in to get a closer look.

"It's a trident," Athena states.

The sight of three men skewered to the sharp trident
prongs held in the slave woman's outstretched hand makes
me uneasy. Nausea sweeps through me as I notice her other
hand is branded with a symbol. I don't need a history lesson
to know it indicates the woman was indeed a slave and
branded as property. however, in that hand, she holds three
trinkets—a coin, a ring, and a compass. I squint to get a
better look.

"You see it, don't you?" asks Athena. "You see the coin in the slave's hand matches the one around your neck."

"Close the book," I tell her. "This coin also matches the one in the catalog you showed me, which means there's probably a treasure trove or at least a hundred of them floating around."

"Yes, but there's a difference," Athena says, staring at my chest again. "Your coin has the loop welded to the top, just like the one in the picture. It was meant to be a keepsake...it was meant to be worn."

"So, it's a knockoff! You're freaking me out," I scoff. "Why are you so interested?"

"Because there's no other story out there like this and I want to be the first to publish it." Athena whines and it frustrates me.

"Publish what? No other story like what?! You want to publish something about treasure and the slave trade?" I question her intently.

"No! About Mermen."

I fall back and slide lower into the hard-wooden library chair and let my head roll back.

I'm not drunk enough for this shit.

"That's how you knew my name," I tell her. "You've been researching my aunt as well."

"Yes," replies Athena. "Your aunt was the expert, so I'm not surprised."

I tilt my head back further to look at the thirty-year-old nerdy librarian whom, I have no doubt, is still a virgin. "She was *not* an expert. She was *crazy*. So, what could possibly surprise you?"

"It doesn't surprise me that *you*, Shelley, would possess and carry at least one of the three trinkets that control the staff of Poseidon, his trident, which is really a metaphor for the three men, or *mer*men, with powers to control the seas."

I think about Blue and squeeze the coin tighter because I know where the coin really came from—a homeless man. The poor guy has probably been in enough trouble, he doesn't need an outlandish crazy woman poking into his business. I already know what that feels like.

"I'm starting to get the feeling you believe in all this stuff, Athena. My aunt labeled herself a psychic, but you should know that 'psychic' is really just another word for *psychotic*."

"Don't you at least find it enthralling? If the legend is true, you hold the fate of the sea along with all who travel upon it, not to mention the fate of a man, who is hundreds of years old, in your hand."

Athena sounds ridiculous. "Don't you mean a *mer*man?" I laugh, but the woman won't give up.

"Listen, after looking at these images, my associates came to the conclusion this was the retelling of a crime of some type. They believe the picture was turned into legend and, as all legends go, it was meant to be a *lesson*. My colleagues believe the three men committed a crime and were cursed for it. They assume the God of the Sea, Poseidon, punished the three men, but I disagree. I think they drowned trying to save this slave aboard this ship. If I've pieced together the legend accurately, to be a merman is not a complete curse. It might sound like a curse because merpeople become isolated and live for centuries without human contact, but it's my understanding it's also a second chance. These three men were granted power by Poseidon, so rather than drown and die, they were transformed. But Poseidon's power ends with the sea. They are creatures of the water that still yearn to walk on land, to be with humans. In order for a merman to return to his human self, he must unite with—"

"Let me guess," I interject, "another element, like a creature of earth, a human."

"Yes!"

"I've heard the rest, Athena."

"Don't you want to know more about the coin?" Athena asks.

"Sure," I say and I know I sound condescending, but it doesn't seem to bring Athena down in the slightest. Her excitement won't quit. Although I've heard portions of this tale before, I do have to wait for Pike because I don't want to walk home in the rain. "Tell me more about the coin."

"The coin controls the merman's fate. I don't know how each trinket is linked to each man, but the person who possesses one of the trinkets has the power to finish the transformation. You have the power to make a man walk again...or *not*. You could force him to sink and swim, which I hope you're not going to do. So, can I ask you again?" Athena takes a breath. "Where'd you get it?"

I can't tell her. If I do, there'll be a whole new can of worms crawling all over my personal investigation to figure out how and when I got the coin along with all the scrapes and bruises. I'm obsessive about unsolved mysteries, which I'm sure has a lot to do with my parents.

There are already too many fish in this fishpond, so I pick up the journal and throw it over to the next table. Athena gasps in horror as she stands up to go get it as I scurry out. I can hear Athena yelling after me as the heavy library doors close and I run onto Main Street.

The rain stopped so the street is again flooded with people who are more excited than they were before the rain. I wonder why Pike didn't come to get me as I look around, but all I see as I spin a few times are wet booties along with people staring at them. Looking for any sign of Pike, I also find myself searching for the stranger who gave me the coin...

Merman.

I'm sure I must be drunk as I spin around like a lunatic

looking for a man I believe could have magical powers that can't speak, can't walk, and claims to have given me this dumb thing around my neck, which might be very valuable, but is causing more trouble than I could wish for, especially since I can't remember a thing about how I got it.

I pause, trying to collect whatever logic I have left and I finally see Pike. He's chatting with a couple of cheeky women under a big tree decorated with lanterns and lights. It makes me ill. I don't care if it was just an extra minute or two, but he left me with Athena for longer than I should've been. I don't want to interrupt his flirty interlude, but I'm ready to go home and I don't mean to Aunt Cora's. I want to go home —back to my messy apartment far away.

I slowly move my feet towards Pike and he sees me. I watch him say farewell to the sassy ladies as I feel something hit the back of my legs. I curse as my body takes flight going backward, but something catches my fall. My bottom lands snugly onto a pair of thighs and I look down to see I've landed in someone's lap.

Pike calls out to me so I turn towards his voice when I see a lightning rod pierce through the night sky hitting the tree he was just under, setting it ablaze. I scream!

I've never been this close to lightning and I'm guessing neither has the rest of the crowd of other booty festival-goers as they join me in a chorus of terror-stricken scream-ing. Pike has one hand on his gun—a trained reaction to loud noises, I figure, and he's watching the flames burning behind him fill the night sky and causing a panic.

I feel a hand wrap around my waist and it's reassuring, so I stop screaming, remaining seated. Everyone else continues to run, cry, and wail as the tree burns as if Heaven sent forth a punishment for behaving like heathens.

I'm quickly spun around and wheeled away, ashamed to peep at the man I'm sitting on. Of course, I know who it is.

I turn back and I see Pike, his face is filled with utter despise knowing he cannot follow me. He must stay, forced to save everyone as he once did me. Pike halfheartedly turns in the opposite direction as I'm rolled away on top of the stranger's lap.

8

BLUE

*T*hat'll teach the sheriff to interfere. I loved the look on his face as I wheeled Shelley away. ·

Shelley. She smells good, but I can't place the scent. It's as if she's dipped herself in a fruity wine—it's intoxicating just breathing her in. I think she might've had a few beers herself. I wish I could to speak her. She hasn't said anything yet, just pointed this way and that as I roll her around. She hasn't even looked at me, which is depressing, and I hope she does not feel indifferent about me because I can't walk.

Of course, she could've gotten off a few blocks ago. Instead, she keeps adjusting herself in my lap. I can tell she's uncomfortable, yet every time she wiggles her arse against my crotch, I get excited and she doesn't seem to mind.

We reach the end of town and hit a dark, seemingly endless, road. This is going to be a long ride and there's no way I'm going to push her that far without her even looking at me. I bite her.

"Ow!" she says rubbing her arm and she finally twists her body to me, still remaining seated. That's good—that she won't get off. "What did you do that for?" she whines.

I stop the chair, cock my head, and motion with my hand from my mouth, encouraging her to speak.

She squints under the moonlight. "You want me to talk?" she replies. I nod and start pushing again. "What do you want me to say?" she mumbles.

I point at her but she turns away, facing forward, and wiggles her bottom in my lap again. *If she keeps this up, I'm going to do more than bite her.*

"I'm not an interesting topic," she shrugs. "I think we should talk about *you*. You're the dark and mysterious one." Her voice softens. "By the way, thank you for taking me home, but I could walk. I'm getting sore sitting like this."

I stop the chair and reach forward to grip her legs. She helps me to turn them sideways, placing them over the side handle, so she's sitting across me in my lap. She smiles and wraps her arm around my back.

"Thanks," she says and grins, finally making eye contact with me. "That's much better."

I push her, carrying her on my lap, for a while in the dark where all I can hear is her breathing and the rolling of the wheels against the smoothed black pavement. I can tell she's thinking about something, deciding what to say, and thank the gods! She finally opens her mouth.

"Where are you from?" she asks.

I look up at the night sky and I find the North Star over the dark horizon. Calculating my position in accordance with the other stars, I point in the direction of England.

"That way?" she asks and I nod. "You're from over there?" she asks again pointing near the same direction, but not exactly and I nod again. Her face looks curious. "You were studying the sky to find your direction. You're a seaman, aren't you?"

I chuckle as I smile and she looks proud of herself.

"So, you're a world traveler?"

I nod then watch her hand as she reaches to her chest, picking up the coin to dangle it in front of me. "You say you gave this to me? Where did you get it from?"

I don't know what to tell her or how. I push the chair a little faster.

"The librarian says this coin is magical. It has magical powers and can control mermen. Have you heard anything about that in all your travels?" she asks.

I still don't know how to respond so I keep pushing us along the side of the road.

"First, you wanted to talk and now you're not responding," she says with a bit of ire behind her tone. I rub the tip of my nose on her arm, which startles her at first, but she calms down. "Sorry," she says. "I don't blame you for not answering. I've had a few too many beers and I'm sure I sound like a crazy person. My aunt used to talk about mermen all the time—it was embarrassing. I thought after she died it would be the end of all the torture, but somehow the issue keeps coming back to haunt me. I feel so stupid just bringing it up."

I stop the chair and lightly grip her chin to turn it towards me. Looking her in the eyes, I shake my head. I want to tell her it's not stupid. I feel her pain—*this is torture!*

"Am I hurting you?" she asks.

I shake my head, *no.*

"I've been in your lap a long time," she says.

I feel the crotch of my pants get tight and I wonder if she even notices what's going on under her thighs.

"I think I'm drunk," she mutters and bats her eyes.

I shake my head, *yes.*

"You're really hot," she says and I had no idea I was giving off such heat.

She kisses me. Traces of booze enter my mouth and I want to get drunk. I wrap my hand around her back and it lands on her plump little arse. I pull her tightly towards me and her entire body leans in as she rubs her hands over the top my head.

She pulls away. "What happened to your hair?" she asks. "Yanka cut it?" I sigh, nod, and start to push. "I like it," she says and I'm relieved. "Do you like her? Do you like Yanka?"

I'm not sure what to say. I *do* like Yanka. She's the first real friend I've had in a long time.

"I have something to confess," Shelley says and my heart beats with anxiousness. "I didn't think much of you until I saw the two of you together. I guess I should've been more open and not so judgmental, but you did try to attack me in the hospital."

I stop pushing and I cringe, shutting my eyes at the thought of what I did. I guess I did scare Shelley climbing up to her wheelchair to get her attention. I figured the moment she saw me, she'd remember how we met and how I saved her.

"Are you okay?" she asks and I open my eyes to look at her face.

I'm not okay. The sight of her makes me not okay. she's so fair, glowing in the moonlight with her hair, curled from the humidity of the air and draped past her shoulders.

There is something too familiar about her. The moment I saw her atop the mountain hiking towards the Peak, I knew we were connected, but I was not okay then. I could not control the thunder or the wind and rain. It was as if the elements took control of me. *She* took control of me and I knew she was the one.

9

SHELLEY

*B*lue doesn't answer. He's looking at me funny, biting his lip as a crack of thunder rips through the sky. I look up. The clouds are rolling in quickly as what little moonlight we had is now dissipating.

"We need to go," I say and I try to get up, but he pulls at my waist. "I think it's going to rain and if I run and you push yourself without me on top of you, maybe we can get to my aunt's house faster."

Blue shakes his head and pushes on his wheels and we start rolling.

"Whoa!" I yell because it scares me a little and he pushes even harder. Rain starts to come down and I have to grip onto him because I feel like I'm going to slip off. I can feel his body shaking up and down—he's laughing!

"Don't laugh!" I snap and he pushes on the wheels with all his might.

I scream louder. My heart takes flight as I cling for dear life as we roll down a slight slant towards Aunt Cora's beach house where there's shelter from all this rain and, hopefully, to where he'll have no choice other than to stay for the night.

I point to the back of the beach house and Blue rolls us around the corner to a ramp as the rain turns into a drizzle. He struggles to roll us both up the ramp. I know his arms are tired and I reluctantly get off and open the door.

"Come in," I tell him as I scamper into the house looking for a towel. I head into the adjacent kitchen and spin around, expecting to see Blue behind me, but he's nowhere to be seen. I skip to the back door and he's still outside with his face pointed upwards to the sky with his mouth open and his tongue hanging out.

"You like the rain. You like getting wet. Don't you?" I ask.

He rolls himself in. He's soaked, along with his chair.

"Wait here," I say and I run around the beach house to get more towels.

When I come back he's got his shirt off and I try not to stare at his muscular upper body slick with rainwater above thin wet jeans that cling to his thighs making the peaks and globes of his groin obvious.

"I think you need to take off your pants before you freeze," I say as I bring him the dry towel. He tries to dry himself off. "Maybe you should move to the couch and I'll see if I can find you something to wear."

Blue wheels himself over to the old, dusty, fluffy couch that's been stuffed, mended, and patched a few hundred times over. I wanted Aunt Cora to throw it away and get a new one, but she insisted it was too comfortable, like a nest handcrafted of multiple materials intended to lure lovebirds.

I leave him to find something to wear in the next room and dig through my backpack. I don't have anything and I don't see any other luggage. I guess I never intended to stay in town more than one or two nights and the rest of my clothes are muddy, which I'd better wash soon.

I move to Aunt Cora's room to look through her stuff and all the old woman's dresses are handmade and too big. I refuse to look like a ragdoll in front of Blue. What's worse is Aunt Cora doesn't own a T-shirt and there's no way I'm going to fit any of her underwear. The only option I have is to wear one of her white tank nightgowns.

I peel off my wet dress and slip on Aunt Cora's nightgown. the neck scoops low—lower than the wet dress I had on, but it works. My nipples are cold and wet and they're obviously hard as they peep through the nightgown so I cross my hands over my chest. I also have nothing underneath, but I'm sure Blue won't even know.

When I come out of Aunt Cora's room, I notice the rain has stopped. It's quiet, except for the sound of the ocean beyond the sand dunes and Blue's heavy breathing.

He made himself comfortable on the couch—the nest made for lovebirds, lying down with his eyes closed and his appendages sprawled over propped pillows. He covered his lower half with a blanket so I tiptoe closer to pull the covers up over him. I flinch as lightning flashes through the windows and thunder creeps through the sky before Blue suddenly grabs my arm.

He slides his back closer to the couch and motions me to lie down with him. I move his chair out of the way and lie down in front of him so he spoons me and covers us both with the blanket. He gingerly moves my hair out of his face and wraps his arm around my body, squeezing me gently.

I listen for more thunder, but all I hear is the air cycling in and out of Blue's lungs as it blows past my ears. It seems to be in sync with the ocean as waves wander upon the sand.

My mind wanders as I close my eyes. I feel like I'm floating over the ocean, but then I start to sink though something won't let me. I open my eyes to see Blue's arm wrapped around me and I pull it tighter, tucking his hand flush around my waist as I close my eyes again.

THE SOUND of chirping resonates in my ears and I open my eyes to the creeping of sunlight inching its way into the beach house. The big glass windows seem eager to greet the sun creeping in between the panes.

My shoulders feel chilly but my toes feel warm and I feel wet heat wafting across my breast and figure I must've turned towards Blue at some point in the night. His arm is still wrapped tautly around me.

I tilt my head down to take a peek at him. My whole breast is hanging out of the neckline of Aunt Cora's over-sized nightgown and Blue's eyes are gaping wide open just staring at it.

I swallow my foul morning breath and try not to move, as my nipple is an inch from his mouth. every breath I take brings my breast closer to his lips. I can't help but take a big breath and my nipple barely brushes across his lower lip.

He looks up at me with bright blue eyes. Neither of us moves for a while. We stare into each other's eyes until he bites his lower lip, which makes my breathing quicken.

I still don't move as he keeps his eyes fixed on mine and I see his tongue slowly reach out of his mouth, past his own lips, and he licks the tip of my nipple. The tiny flicker of his tongue over the small mound at the tip of my tit sends a shockwave throughout my body.

I swallow again, but I can't keep it in. "Just bite it," I whisper.

Blue breaks eye contact and latches his mouth over my breast and then grabs at my thigh, pulling it over his side. I moan as he licks and sucks, moving his hand between my legs and up my thigh until he reaches my slick folds, spreading them and plunging his digit into me.

"Oh God!" I cry as he plunges two fingers in and out, deeper and deeper, until his fingers climb out and he finds the small mound that is meant to make me peak with pleasure. He rubs my clit and I cannot contain myself. My back arches as he rubs and sucks on my nipple until I fall backward—halfway off the couch with my head on the floor as he grips my leg.

I start laughing and tilt my head up to see Blue peek over the couch, but he's not laughing. He keeps gripping on the one leg and wraps it behind him. He leans over my hips that are still on the couch and spreads my pussy lips open. His tongue darts out to lick me and I'm in ecstasy, but my head hanging upside down feels heavy. The feeling is familiar and the image of a man with a fishtail swims by in my head. Alarming, but it turns me on.

Blue continues to move his tongue softly as I allow the fantasy of the man with the fishtail to take over my mind. As the space between my legs starts to soak of Blue's saliva, I imagine an ocean and Blue as a merman licking at my clit. I'm drenching him in my come as I explode on his face.

I envision Blue with a long, shiny fishtail pulling me out of the water with my legs dragging until they touch the sand and then both of us in the sun as he squeezes himself between my legs. I can almost feel the waves washing over my toes. it brings me back to Blue's tongue as it swishes and swashes over my clit that is beginning to reach its summit.

My leg clamps around him and Blue swirls his whole head a bit faster. I moan and his tongue swirls so fast, it feels like my clit is caught in a violent vortex so heavy and wet making me so ready to come.

Blue shoots his finger into my canal and, like lightning, it sends off a chain reaction and I groan. He plunges his digit deeper and pushes in harder, helping me to climb towards my peak and I feel my voice sounds off like a siren as I come on Blue's tongue.

He continues swirling his tongue, sending shockwaves throughout my body until I cannot stand the pleasure anymore. I push away, feeling silly for wanting him to be a merman and he tries to grip my thighs, but I escape his hands as I let the lower half of my limp body slip off the couch and onto the floor.

Blue peeps over the edge. I cannot see his legs as I'm still imagining he has a fishtail. I feel so irrational, like a naïve high school girl with her head in the clouds imagining a merman wrapped between her legs. Yes, I used to have those thoughts, but I do *not* want to know what Blue would think of me if he knew.

I collect myself and stand up to grab Blue's clothes for him as he sits up. He's mostly naked except for the corner of the blanket that covers his package and I notice how thin his legs are compared to the average man. He's still adorably sexy and my mind wanders to the size of his package. Though he's disabled from the waist down, maybe his stuff doesn't work, but I'm tempted to find out.

I hand him the clothes Yanka dressed him in even though they are still damp, but he doesn't mind in the least. He's able to dress himself. I keep my eyes above his waist whenever I try to offer him help as he struggles a bit, but he indicates with pointed fingers and a raised hand, several times, he wants to do it on his own. His legs seem stronger than they were and I see he's able to put a little bit of weight on them to help him pivot from the sofa and into the wheelchair.

Blue pushes himself towards me, proud of himself for getting dressed and I'm sure for giving me an orgasm, as he rolls himself a few feet in my direction. I'm about to ask him if he'll take me for another ride on his wheelchair, but I'm distracted by another set of wheels also rolling in our direction. Through the window, I see dust stirring behind Pike's police car as he speeds towards us with his lights flashing— another big storm is on the way.

10

BLUE

*S*helley looks disturbed. I watch her eyes as they follow something, or someone, through the window and towards the front door until we hear a pounding.

"Shelley!" yells the Sheriff. "You got that stranger in there? Open up!"

Shelley hesitates. I want to tell her not to open it, in hopes he'll go away. I'm sure he's jealous, but I can't speak a word and she goes to open the door.

The sheriff pushes himself in, like an arse, and tosses Shelley aside.

"You!" he says pointing at me and marches towards me.

Shelley cries as she grabs the sheriff's arm that is reaching for the shackles hanging at his waist. "What are you doing?!"

The sheriff pushes her and she falls. As I reach towards her, the sheriff reaches to his hip and pulls out a gun. I know guns. I've seen them multiply in numbers and evolve as fast as humans have, but their purpose has not changed. All guns do are drown lads in their own blood.

"Put your hands behind your back," he says and I know this drill. He's shackled me once before.

Shelley is crying. "Pike, what are you doing?! He's been with me the whole night."

I'm just as surprised as she is but her words matter not, as the sheriff tugs hard at my arms, purposefully trying to hurt me as he shackles my wrists.

"I'm sorry to tell you this, Shelley, but while your stranger was in the hospital I took the liberty of collecting some DNA samples and had Athena send them to the university where they do our forensic testing." The sheriff yanks on the shackles to make sure they're tight.

"So?" she asks.

"Our stranger's hair matches one of the hairs on your parents' boat we found anchored and abandoned at sea."

"What? That doesn't make any sense. That was twenty years ago! My Aunt Cora said—"

"Your Aunt Cora lied," snickers the sheriff. "She asked us all to lie to you when you were a child, but since you insist on harboring a potential criminal, I think you should know your parents' boat was found in the company of another smaller paddle boat reportedly stolen. Neither your father or your mother, despite all our diving efforts, were nowhere to be found nor were there any traces of your parents, other than the blood we found along the deck determined to be your mother's."

I gulp. I don't understand how the sheriff pieced together the story, but I do know what he is talking about. I also know why Shelley looks so familiar and how and why we are connected.

My heart sinks. If I had known and made the connection beforehand, I would've never chosen to behave like an angler —desperate to enjoy the trappings of a woman, especially *this* woman.

"We also found a strand of hair," continues the sheriff, "that matches the one from your friend here."

"That's ridiculous! You're lying. You set this up, Pike! You can't arrest him because you're jealous."

The sheriff pushes me in the wheelchair to the front door. "Don't flatter yourself, Shelley. You've certainly grown up to be beautiful, but you're as loony as the rest of the women in your family."

"Fuck you!" she cries and the wooden floor shakes as she stomps towards us, attempting to strike the sheriff.

"Cut this out right now," he says as he blocks her, but she's able to get in a good smack to his neck with the other hand. "Goddamnit, Shelley!" he shouts as he pushes her back forcing her to hit a wall, but it doesn't stop her.

Shelley charges the sheriff again and I want to tell her to stop. I want to tell her to leave him alone. The sight of her in distress and using her hands to fight for what she wants is too familiar. *She looks exactly like her father.*

The gobsmacked sheriff takes another slap and if I don't do something, she's going to get hurt. If she's anything like her father, she's going to keep fighting and arguing until she gets what she wants and I can't let her fight for me. I *know* she's fighting for me, but I can't let her go on like this. Not for me.

I look at the five steps of steep stairs leading down the front door and I lift myself off the seat of the wheelchair. I make an attempt to stand up. I can't believe it—I'm on my two feet!

Wobbling as every muscle in my body, including my arms and back, work in unison to keep me upright, I hear Shelley shout. "Catch him!"

For a moment, I regret doing this. I'm about to land on my face and arms atop of a hardwood stairwell painted the color of the seashore. I hit the steps hard and my body stumbles down to the ground.

Pike shows no mercy for the pain I'm in. I taste blood in my mouth from piercing my tongue with my own teeth, but the pain of Pike pulling me up by my arms and the embarrassment of not being able to stand on my own hurts more than anything.

"You stupid fuck," the sheriff states as he drags me across the dry rubble and towards the car. Opening the back door, he tries to lift me, but struggles. "Get in the car," he says.

I see Shelley coming towards us. She's screaming at the top of her lungs. I can't even make out what she's saying. Her hair is not as red, but she is as irrational as her father and my heart sinks deeper into my gut.

The sheriff tries to pick me up and I wrap my shackled wrists around his neck to help him as he loads me into the car. He shuts the door, walks around the enclosed metal carriage, and gets in as Shelley continues to spit fire. I think even the sheriff is afraid of the flames pouring out of her mouth.

"Pike, you fucking asshole! Get him out of the car!" she screams as she pounds on the door.

I see the sheriff work a few gadgets and knobs with his hands and a rumbling resounds, vibrating straight through the cushioned seat and into my bones. It has the same sound as speedy boats that have lost their sails. In truth, I've always wanted to ride in one of these—*a car*, but not under these circumstances. I'm sure a sheriff's job is the same as it was back in the days before I had fins.

I'm sure I'm going to jail, but I hope I won't have to face a hanging.

11

BLUE

"*Y*ou just can't seem to stay out of trouble, can you?" Yanka asks as she props her head against the cell door.

I spin my chair around over the smooth, freshly mopped floor of the jail cell, which comes complete with a firm bed and a whirlpool for the biggies that come out of my arse. *This is hardly the gallows.*

"What happened to you, Blue?" she whines, slipping her fingers through a small rectangular hole below a glass window in the door. "I've been looking everywhere for you and then I found out this morning Sheriff Pike arrested you."

"He's being held for suspicion of murder," says a female voice and a redhead looms from beyond the meshed door.

"There's no way! Blue is not the type to commit murder. Believe me, I know," Yanka defends me and I'm glad she has so much confidence in me as she flashes a smile. Yanka then looks back to the redhead with disdain, "And who the fuck are you?"

"I'm Athena," the woman says with pride, but Yanka shakes her head and continues to stare wide-eyed at Athena who's face falls morose. "I'm the librarian, also named the town historian and assistant to the Sheriff's Department." Yanka continues to shake her head as she surveys Athena. Athena slouches. "I moved here two years ago, Illuyanka. We've crossed paths a few times."

"Honey, I have no idea who you are," smirks Yanka, "and if you *did* you'd know not to call me by my full name. *Nobody* calls me by that name."

"Illuyanka? Because it means 'seadragon?'"

"No!" Yanka shouts and I laugh to myself as Yanka's features soften and her eyes grow with inquisition. "Seadragon. Is that really what my name means?"

Athena chuckles, "Yes. Illuyanka was derived from Hittite mythology and is often depicted as a serpentine."

"I thought you said it meant dragon!"

"In ancient cultures, both serpent and dragon could mean the same thing."

"Whatever." Yanka rolls her eyes. "Tell me again why you're here. Are you going to help him?"

I roll my chair a little closer to the door, suspecting Athena is working with the sheriff to find good cause to hang me.

Athena's eyes wander over me, studying my legs and the chair through the glass before fixing her glasses. When she catches me blankly staring back, she flushes with embarrassment to have been caught examining me without my permission.

"Sheriff Pike is having difficulty piecing together his case," Athena tells Yanka. "A strand of Mr. Doe's—"

"Blue!" corrects Yanka. "His name is Blue."

"Okay," Athena says with a quibble in her voice and looks back in my direction studying me again. "A sample of *Blue's* hair matches evidence once removed from the scene of a suspected crime about twenty years ago, but it's clear this man would've been a child back then."

"What crime?!" shouts Shelley coming down the hall.

I roll my chair up to the door until my toes touch so I can see her coming, but I can't see her, as I'm seated too low. I hear her wooden, sandaled feet pacing down the hall and I try to call out to her, but only air wafts through my throat.

Fuck. It's been three hundred years and I'm still trying to use a voice I do not have. But I need to tell Shelley the truth. I need to tell her she shouldn't listen to any of this because the only person who knows the truth about what happened to her parents is me. I also want to apologize and, although I'm not innocent, I've been absolved of my sins.

"I'm sorry, Shelley, I probably shouldn't talk about Blue's case with you," says Athena.

I finally see Shelley as she comes in view through the window and she doesn't even look at me. She flicks her long, strawberry blonde hair and puts one fair hand on her hip as the other points a finger in Athena's face. "If it involves Blue and my parents, then you're going to tell me everything you know."

"Shelley's right, Athena," interrupts Yanka. "You're new here and—"

"I've lived here for two years!" cries Athena, which Yanka doesn't appear to appreciate. Yanka sticks her large chest out pushing the redhead back a few inches. Athena clutches her notes, intimidated between the two women and the three of them together remind me of my two brothers and me.

Of course, we were not born as brothers but *became* brothers—first by wind as navigators of the sea, then by a fire aboard a burning ship, and again by keepers of the sea. As of late, we are not so close as we once were, each eager to be free of our aqueous realm and return to earth, to land. If that should cost us our brotherhood, so be it. We have sailed, fought, died, and bickered together for too long.

As the women—Yanka, Athena, and Shelley squabble among themselves, I comprehend why Poseidon loves women so much. he adores them. He disguises himself to entice them and then trick them into lying with him. He goes as far as to allocate his powers to mortal men, like my brothers and me, which gives him more time to pursue the pleasures of women.

It is not surprising his name, Poseidon, should mean "husband to earth," because he listens to women, too, as they complain, and he often becomes inclined to aid their cries. In truth, a woman's wailing is Poseidon's weakness. if a woman should pray to him to save her from whatever darkness haunts her at sea, he will send forth the lightning, waves, and the beasts of the ocean to save her. These things I know—*I am* his lightning.

But Poseidon cannot save every feminine creature that cries to him, one of his many regrets, for on occasion, some women wish for death. Poseidon would easily kill a man at his own request, but he pities the woman who is in so much pain she should wish her fate to end sooner than destiny would allow. It's these women whom Poseidon fights the most to understand, to nurture, and to win their affections and love. So, rather than simply grant a woman's dying wish, he strips her of her humanity and elevates her to the status of sea goddess, or sea witch, granting her powers and dominion over others.

Most times it works against him and he ends up quarreling with them for all eternity because witches are hellbent on achieving nothing but revenge. Yet, I believe Poseidon enjoys bickering with goddesses of the sea. Looking at these three women bickering amongst themselves —the healer, the scholar, and the survivor, they are each a goddess of their own making and I pray Poseidon should never get a hold of the one that holds my love.

Shelley, I sense, possesses no super existential power other than the simple human state her mortal parents gave her. Apart from the fire that spews from her mouth when she is speaking in anger, which I suspect also fuels the slight red tint to her hair, Shelley is of pure earth and she's used that earth to build a shell around her for protection. It's allowed her to survive in the harsh environment of human ridicule, but inside, she is soft—and it drives me mad.

I want to fondle every bit of her soft, fleshy, pink mortal skin between her legs with my tongue and bite the sweet plump earthly fruit of her bum as well as her breasts. Even more, as the earth cradles the water that rests upon it, I wish to be cradled, to rest in the protective shell of her arms where I know no other human or god can make me feel anything less than a man.

I knock on the cell door, but not one of three hears me.

"Tell me what you know about my parents' death!" Shelley bellows at Athena.

"I already told you I can't," argues Athena back at her.

Shelley steps back for a moment, thinking, as she spins around. She grips the coin around her neck and dangles it in front of Athena's face and the scholar's eyes widen. "Tell me everything you know and I'll give you this coin."

Lightning strikes outside and I bang on the door so hard it scares the three of them because it is louder than the thunder rolling through the halls. I shake my head at Shelley. Her face is blank as if she lost all feeling for me, but I do feel another one of the three looking at me much too inquisitively for her own good.

Athena is studying me, eyeing me up and down with her squinted, beady eyes framed behind her scholarly spectacles. She holds her palm beneath the dangling coin. "I will tell you everything you want to know if you give me the coin *and* also tell me where it came from."

"Give the coin to Athena," Yanka states and another crack of lightning strikes the earth, but it doesn't keep Yanka from continuing to convince Shelley of giving up the coin. "Honestly, Shelley, you're not the only one who's been haunted by the thought of your missing parents for the last twenty years. I know you had a hard time growing up with all the gossip about hungry sea monsters or worse, human traffickers. And, I'm not trying to tell you what to do, but if the book nerd says she can help you find out the truth, I think we'll all be better off getting some answers."

Another bolt of lightning strikes as the coin slips from Shelley's hand into Athena's palm. "Speak," Shelley demands and I feel an ache in my toes.

Athena puts the coin around her neck and I feel the ache spread up into my spine. I bang on the cell door once more with my hands and shake my head wildly. Gripping onto the top of my wheels, I push forward, banging my feet atop the footrests against the door wildly.

Yanka puts her forehead to the glass again. "Don't worry, baby, I'm sure there's some clue that's going to help get you out of there. Let the psycho and the nerd figure it out, okay?"

Athena flips open one of the folders in her hand and skims over the pages. "Shelley, you know your mother was committed to a psychiatric facility for a week before they figured out she had mercury poisoning."

"No," Shelley gulps. "I didn't know. I know some people say she was crazy. How'd she get mercury poisoning?"

"From eating too much fish," replies Yanka. "This *is* a fishing town."

Athena smiles, "Yes, but that's not all of it. Your mother, Shelley, as you know was a geologist, a volcanologist to be exact. She traveled often before settling here with your father."

"I know this," says Shelley. "What about the mercury?"

"It poisoned her. It most likely got into her system working around volcanoes and eating a lot of deep-sea fish, but who knows what else. There are tons of mercury hazards that find their way into the human body, like fluorescent light bulbs, for example. But I'm sure it was a combination of things that contributed to a rise in mercury levels in your mother's blood. Did you know in the 1700s, women wore blush with mercury in it and they had no idea they were poisoning themselves, contributing to neurological disorders, madness, and even death?"

I know what Athena is talking about. When I was a seaman, I saw men who ate too much deep-sea fish become looney, like the women who wore too much red rouge. They became sick in the head, scratching at their cheeks until they eventually peeled their own skin from their face, nearly bleeding to death. But it wasn't just the scraping of her visage. When I saw Shelley's mother with a knife in her hand, alone at sea, I never knew she had poison in her blood.

"What else?" asks Shelley. "What about my father?"

"We don't know much about your father other than he was a geologist, too. He studied rocks and loved your mother."

Shelley grins. "My Aunt Cora said my father loved my mother *too* much. My aunt said he'd cut out his own heart, give up an arm and a leg, do anything for her, go anywhere to be with her."

Shelley's right. Her father did say he'd do anything for her. He'd give up everything to be with the woman he loved. In fact, he did. he died traveling to the depths of the sea just to be with his wife, though I had no idea he'd given up his own daughter.

"So, what more?" asks Shelley. "What about the suspected crime?"

"Your parents' boat was found anchored with blood across the deck with a paddle boat tied to the back. There were no signs of your parents other than the blood, which they tested and found to match your blood and figured it had to be your mother's. They sent divers but could not find any sign of either of your parents. There was a bit of lightning, but no storm reported that night and there was no reported call for help."

"Tell me about the hair," inquires Shelley.

"They found a single strand of hair, which has been preserved as evidence. It never matched a soul until now."

All three goddesses look at me.

"Blue," Shelley says softly, bringing her forehead to the door. "Do you know anything about this?"

"How could he know anything about this?" asks Yanka. "Look at him! He couldn't have been more than ten years old. Do you think a ten-year-old could've paddled out to sea and killed a couple of adults and then swim a few miles back to shore? How could he be responsible for a couple of missing people, let alone your parents?"

I close my eyes and cringe at what I did, knowing I *am* responsible. I'm not responsible for everything that happened, for the deaths of *both* of Shelley's parents, but I am responsible for killing one.

"You do know something," Shelley mumbles. She slips her fingers through the hole in the door to reach for me. "Tell me what it is."

I'm afraid to look at her. I love her, but at this moment, I'm afraid to look at the likeness of both her mother and father. I still do not regret what I did, but Shelley may never forgive me and I might never walk again.

"Goddamnit, Blue!" Shelley yells and pounds on the glass. "Tell me what happened!"

"Hey!" yells Sheriff Pike from down the hall. "None of you are supposed to be here. How the hell did you girls get in?"

"I flashed the deputy my tits," says Yanka, "but I don't know how the other two got in."

Athena fixes her glasses. "There was no one at the desk when I came by."

"That's because he was probably pleasuring himself after he got a good look at these," replies Yanka cupping her big breasts and I'm surprised she chose to be a healer. She'd probably make more than a few pretty pennies as a harlot.

"Tell me what you know, Blue," continues Shelly. Her voice is low, like a deep-sea creature swooping in right before it makes its kill. I haven't heard her speak in this tone before.

"He can't speak," Yanka iterates. "How's he going to tell you?"

The sheriff grips Shelley by the arm and pulls her to face him. "He's not going to tell you even if he could talk because he's a murderer and criminals don't easily give up their secrets. Now, the three of you need to get the hell out of here!"

"But you asked for my help," says Athena to the sheriff.

"That didn't include questioning witnesses related to the case. That's *my* job," he replies, "so get out and I'll call you when you're needed."

The three of them are reluctant to leave and I hate to see Shelley depart with her heart wide open and wanton of answers to questions only I can answer, but cannot speak.

1 2

SHELLEY

"*Y*ou still owe me," Athena informs me as she catches up from behind.

"What are you talking about?"

"I gave you every piece of information I had about your parents' case in exchange for the coin *and* the name of the person who gave it to you."

I stop in my tracks. There's already too much confusion and Athena is too much of a fantasy fanatic to handle the truth.

"I can't tell you," I turn to say then I keep going.

Athena grabs my arm, gripping it tight. "But you said you'd give me the coin and—"

"I know what I said!" I snap. "But to be honest, the information you gave me was hardly worth giving you the entire coin in addition to the information you want."

"Why is it such a secret?" she whines. "Who are you protecting?"

"Ya know? For a book nerd, you're not very bright. I'm surprised you haven't figured it out yet."

I take a few steps down the sidewalk and I notice Athena

is not following me. Turning around, I see Athena standing in the middle of the sidewalk like she's stuck in a trance as she rubs at the coin around her neck with her fingertips.

I walk back towards her because I know the wheels are turning in that nerdy brain of hers and she's up to no good. I've known way too many fanatics in my lifetime so I recognize the crazy shit they are capable of thinking and doing.

As I open my mouth to speak, Athena cuts me off, "We need to get him out," she says.

"Who? The murderer?" Yanka questions as she catches up. I huff and cross my arms.

"No, the *merman*," Athena replies.

"You're fucking crazy," I say.

Yanka starts laughing. "You're both fucking crazy, but if you're planning on busting Blue out, I'll help you. Anything to piss off Pike and move Blue back in with me. I'm good at hiding things from the authorities."

Athena rolls her eyes. "Blue gave the coin to Shelley," Athena says, fixating her eyes and pointer finger on me. "He *chose* you, Shelley. After everything you've been taught and everything you've been through, how can you not believe in him? How can you not want to help him?"

"He's not a fucking *merman*, Athena!" I snap. "You sound like my aunt!"

"So, how did you get the coin?" Yanka asks me and I hope she's not buying into all this merman business because if she is she's going to be even more desperate for him.

I admit, "I can't remember."

"You'd better remember," threatens Yanka. "If that thing is linked to him, to his past and who he is, then how did you get it? It was on you when you arrived at the hospital and, according to the doc, he nearly attacked you for it. And you can't remember?"

I don't remember, but I do recall my ride home on the

seat of his lap as his arms worked hard to push the two of us all the way to Aunt Cora's beach house. I remember how terrible I felt when I thought the worst of him and how sexy I thought he was after he got me off with his tongue.

Now, I think the worst of him again while Yanka and Athena are willing to do anything for him and continuing only to think the very best of him.

Why? How is it they can so easily give themselves up so quickly without knowing who he really is?

At the very least, I remember how excruciating it hurt when I found out my parents were never coming home. As a child, I wished every day since then a merman had, indeed, taken them to paradise together as Aunt Cora speculated.

Yanka is right. I need to remember, not just because this disabled man could be innocent, but also because he's linked to my parents somehow and I need to find out why and how.

I look at the coin on Athena's neck and I regret giving it to her. "I'll help you," I say. "I'll help you both get Blue out of prison."

It's been raining since yesterday. Despite the air-conditioning, it still feels muggy inside of Yanka's car. It's as if there's no remedy for the humidity and I wish I had a better part in this prison break besides watching and waiting in the driver's seat.

I can't believe I'm doing this.

Athena thinks we'll be able to stroll him right out. She knows where the security recordings are, which she will delete and disable, as well as where they keep the keys to the cells. She says she knows the police station well after going in and out to help the sheriff with cases. Athena mentioned she's been the sheriff's go-to girl for research and cataloging evidence and he uses her connections with the university, so he trusts her. Athena will be the one to open the cell and I think she really should've been a detective, but the way she dresses—like a librarian, says she's hardly the type to get involved with criminals...*but then again, here we are.*

Yanka's job is to distract the deputy. She says she's willing to go as far as letting him grope her tits, especially since the deputy has had a hard crush on her ever since he came into the hospital room accompanying some kid he found a few years back with a broken arm after falling out of a tree. I don't know why Yanka doesn't date the deputy. He's hot— short blonde hair, green eyes, and a tan to boast. But I figure Yanka won't date him because the deputy is not the type of guy who needs saving. Yanka has a serious problem with being attracted to things desperate for her help.

I feel a patch of heat melting my forearm and I look down to see sunlight beaming on my skin. Looking down at my outfit, it's stained brown in a few spots, which I couldn't wash out, so I figure I had to have been hiking and fallen at some point. Beyond that, I see my boots. I know I used them recently, but I can't remember. If I'd known I'd be in on a heist, I would've brought tennis shoes from my apartment since my boots will weigh me down if we need to run for some reason.

The sunshine blares brighter and the rain has come to a sparse drizzle when I hear a knock at the window. it's Athena waving her arms around frantically. I guess I locked the door.

Unlocking the car, I can't help but notice the coin dangling around Athena's neck as she opens the back door and pushes Blue's wheelchair as close as she can. Helping him to get inside, she quickly folds the collapsible wheelchair Yanka took from the hospital. When I see Blue struggling to get in, my stomach churns. Not only do I realize what we've just done, but I also feel like I've been horrible to him.

I know why Athena wants him—she's obsessed with testing out her theory of throwing him into the water from Yanka's boat, which is where Yanka, however, is planning to keep him. But Athena thinks if she throws him overboard, Blue will grow fins and swim and she'll have made the discovery of the century.

Yanka wants him because she thinks by rescuing him, he'll be forever indebted to her and she can add him to her collection of adoring critters who have nothing but an incomprehensible and unfathomable I-will-never-leave-you type of love for her. Plus, he's sexy and he can't run away from her.

Me? I just want the truth. After I have it, I plan to leave him on the boat and send him on his way, back to wherever it is he came from.

Athena guarantees we won't get caught. There's already evidence of all of us at the prison earlier, so there should be nothing else to link us to the break, except Yanka's presence, but the deputy feeling up her titties will be her alibi.

As I see Yanka scuttling out of the station, I start up the engine. Yanka gets into the backseat with Blue and I take off, trying not to peel away too quickly or attract any unwanted attention. Athena was right. We *were* able to just walk in and roll Blue right out of the sheriff's department.

"I can't believe we just busted a man out of prison," I say driving us out of town and down a winding back road.

"This is a small town with simple minds," Athena says. "I told you if we behaved like everything was normal, no one would suspect anything fishy is going on."

"If Pike finds out it was us, he'll go to jail for murdering us himself," I say.

"Don't worry," Athena reassures as she glances back to Blue, "I've put in a failsafe."

"What are you talking about?" I ask.

"I left traces of evidence from smugglers who came through last year in the cell. They'll think Blue is linked to them and they kidnapped him somehow."

"But if he is found that'll get him in more trouble!" snaps Yanka.

"He's not going to be found because we are taking him back to the sea. Isn't that right?" asks Athena as she turns around from the passenger seat to look at Blue.

Yanka starts arguing with her because we clearly did not think this through. It hurts my ears but I just keep driving. I do on occasion peep back at Blue. he is staring at me through the rear-view mirror with those two big blue oceans of eyes. Somewhere, deep within them, I know he's hiding something. somehow I'm going to make him talk.

13

BLUE

*S*he keeps staring at me. I wish I could say it's because she feels the same way I do—we are connected. But deep down, I know she wants answers and she's suspicious I'm somehow responsible for her fate, which in part, I am.

All three of them help me get onto the boat. If my brothers could see me now, I'm sure they'd be jealous. Nevertheless, I fear Poseidon could be watching us right now as well. I'm sure he'd punish me by making me a sea slug or bottom-feeding flatfish for having these three mortal goddesses at my disposal.

Yanka cranks a few gadgets on the boat deck and it rumbles. Athena begins cheering as we take off with Yanka steering us into the sunset. They each take turns looking at me, hoping the others won't see. I don't think they have any idea what they plan to do with me, but I do know they each want something from me.

We haven't traveled long when a wave hits the front of the boat and splashes high over the deck, causing the women to scream. It's come out of nowhere and I know one of my brothers, the Captain, who is also the custodian of the waters of the sea, has found me.

"Where did that come from?" Yanka asks and I see Athena is soaked. She's glaring at me with a wickedly curious eye.

The boat tips to the side a little and all three women scream again as my chair tips just slightly then lands back on two wheels.

"It's a whale!" cries Shelley with excitement and I'm thrilled to see her smiling again.

I can't help but laugh as the women stop screaming and start wooing with the sight of a second sea ocean creature, an adolescent humpback, who decides to show off as it breaches in the air.

The adolescent swims close and shoots a spout of water towards the sky, which comes down over the boat showering Athena's white blouse. her thin undergarments expose her exquisite mortal body, which she's always trying to hide.

The adolescent splashes his tail against the surface of the water and I know my other brother, once a Master at Arms and now a Master of Sea Beasts, has found me as well.

Pushing my wheelchair to the edge of the boat, I want my brothers to see my legs. It doesn't matter my legs don't work well. I'm sure it will give them hope.

"You did this!" Athena claims and I can't tell if she's happy or angry she's soaked and dripping with seawater. "You can control elements of the sea." She attempts to pull me out of the chair, but I resist. I think she's planning to throw me overboard.

Yanka stops the boat and comes rushing over. "What the hell are you doing?"

"I'm going to toss him in!"

"Are you crazy?" replies Yanka. "He'll fucking drown!"

"He's a merman!" Athena remarks as she tries to tug harder, nearly knocking me out of the chair.

Yanka turns to Shelley who is just watching, which I don't understand. "Help me," Yanka begs her. "Help me before Athena drowns him!"

"Why are you so desperate to believe he's a merman, Athena?" asks Shelley. "I once believed as you did, but I grew out of that. You're older than me. You've got to be what? Thirty-something? Why would anyone continue to believe in all this folklore? You're willing to risk a man's life to prove a theory in which no truth exists."

"Because they *do* exist," says Athena, "I've seen one."

"Ah fuck!" cries Yanka. "You people are driving me crazy. Listen to me," she snaps. "I'm not a psychiatric nurse. I work in the emergency and surgical rooms of the hospital. I don't know how to handle your mental bullshit."

"So, you're saying you've seen Blue before?" Shelley inquires with complete disregard for Yanka's pleas and Athena shakes her head.

"No," Athena replies and lets go of my arm to sit at the edge of the boat sulking.

"Then tell me why you think Blue is a merman," Shelley urges.

Athena lifts the coin from her neck to dangle it in front of her eyes. "Because this town, Porterman's Bluff, is haunted," she says looking at Shelley. "You've heard the stories. I've been able to put them together, but it's Cora Morae's story, your aunt's tale, which was passed down through generations that makes me believe things I saw in my youth were not fantasy, but reality."

I see the other two women become weak in the knees as the boat rocks back and forth, forcing them to also take a seat.

"Tell me, Athena," says Shelley with her green eyes fixed on me. "Tell me the story my aunt, the crazy psychic, told you as she taught me many things, but she never mentioned any hauntings."

Athena begins to tell her tale and I'm amazed at how true it is for having been passed between generations in the Morae family. She doesn't know every detail, but what she does know, is every bit as I remember...

Before America's revolution was won, I was a low-ranking, illiterate seaman aboard a British Royal Naval ship. I was lucky at the time to be assigned under Captain Willis Sturgeon, a fine commander who was also an exceptional navigator. His best friend, Orphelius Mayhem, a Master at Arms, was among the finest sailors I'd ever had the chance to work under, but they weren't just naval men—they were warriors. They enjoyed plundering, almost like pirates, by taking part in as many a good fight as possible, regardless of whether it was on land or by sea.

Furthermore, they loved their women, but not as much as the women loved them. Heroic tales of Captain Willis and Master Mayhem allowed for the easy trappings of many a pretty lady. Women waited with preceding tales of heroism on every corner of the earth for these men, and these men did not discriminate against any of the women. It didn't matter if a woman was a harlot or an aristocrat, pink or pale, thin or oppositely thick, these two men loved their women and they reveled in being worshipped by all kinds.

I wanted to be like them. I wanted to be exactly like the brawny Captain Willis and the slender, dark-eyed devil with a sword—Master Mayhem. I coveted to be every bit of a hero as they were and when the night finally arrived to prove I could be, I paid the price for my heroics. we three each continue to pay the price.

We were aboard the Annabelle, a fine ship, with a mission to protect another carrying ammunition to the coast of the Americas. Annabelle was newly commissioned so most of its crew was recently thrown together. On a warm, windless night, we sat atop a motionless sea. The stars were brighter than ever and the atmosphere was so quiet, you could hear a man breathing from the opposite deck. But what should've been a blissful night of sleep and peace made us all uneasy as a woman wailed for hours from the opposite boat. We had an idea of what was happening to her and it was confirmed the next day when our skipper, Captain Willis, boarded the other vessel insisting its captain cease exploiting the handful of African female slaves aboard the ship. Captain Willis initially seemed pleased with himself, thinking he had made an impact to put us all at ease, but rumors shortly spread of his uneasiness about one particular slave.

Unfortunately, on the next evening, we heard a woman wailing again, except this time she was shrieking between cries as if the other captain was making an example of her. Slave or no slave, it made my blood curdle and I did not want to imagine the torture she must've endured.

So again the next morning, Captain Willis returned to the opposite ship in an attempt to bring the abused slave back to our boat, reporting he wasn't interested in saving her, but simply couldn't sleep. Witnesses aboard the ship say the slave professed to be a witch and cursed our captain and everyone in his company. They claimed she implored the gods to strike down all who boarded the boat. Captain Willis, feeling inept at trying to save an ungrateful woman, left her to endure more torture.

On the third night, we were not just awoken by the sound of the slave woman's lamenting but by the screaming of many. I recall the sound of thunder as lightning struck the ship, which soon lit up with flames. Fueled by the fury of the wind and not a drop of rain in sight, the fire grew so high it filled the entire sky.

Captain Willis called on all hands to attempt a rescue. We

brought our ship around as close as we could and dropped two rescue boats into the water. Captain Willis was upset to see only the officers were aboard when the rescue boats returned. There was clearly room for more passengers, as well as a portion of her majesty's property, which soon sunk. Screams were heard from the burning vessel as the officers, including Captain Averill Porterman from the opposite ship, were hoisted to safety.

The captains argued about the lack of judgment, but ultimately Captain Willis called for two brave men to follow him back to save what he could. His closest friend, Master Orphelius Mayhem, and I volunteered, of course.

I remember thinking how foolish I was as I climbed down the rope to follow behind them onto the rescue boat. I could feel the heat and hot ash flying past me and doubted, for a moment, about going until Captain Willis shouted to me, "Push us off, brother! Let us revel for a moment with our oars, so we may celebrate as heroes rewarded by our whores!"

Master Mayhem laughed as he grabbed his oar and I discovered inexperienced feelings buried deep within me. As I pushed us off, I peered at the good captain leading us towards danger, but I was not afraid. I found courage I never knew I had and felt invincible in the presence of these heroic men.

As I struggled to climb the rope to the top rear deck of the burning ship, I nearly let go as an explosion set off by ammunition sent pieces of flaming debris past me. Luckily, Master Mayhem put his hand out and pulled me to the top of the chaotic scene.

I followed the Captain and the Master at Arms, both fearless and determined as they headed towards the steps to get below deck. I suspected once there they would head in the direction of her majesty's loot, but they did not. Instead, they followed the wail of the woman who cursed him earlier. When we found her, shackled, the flames were almost upon her.

Captain Willis and Master Mayhem worked frantically to free her. They called to me to look for a key, so I headed out of the slave quarters in search of one, only to find myself in the ammunition room.

Within seconds of entering, there was an explosion. I remember the feeling of the initial blast. My body was numb, but not my throat. It was as if I swallowed fire. I could not breathe—my lungs and throat were instantly burned. I remember seeing water pour through the hull from a hole in the side of the ship until it flooded the room.

I was still attempting to make my way out when I was consumed by the ocean. stuck in the ship that was becoming my coffin. I was going down with it. I remember trying desperately to scrape at the wood with my fingertips. My last feeling as a human was that of a splinter wedged beneath my nail when suddenly *I could breathe*, but it was *not* through my nose.

Still, I was relieved until I felt an excruciating pain in my legs as though a fishing line was cutting straight through them. When I looked down, I saw it was my trousers cutting through my legs as my bones began to crack. Removing my trousers promptly, I watched my skin somewhat melt as the flesh of my inner legs fused together. I tried to scream, but I was voiceless in an ocean tomb. I continued to attempt to bellow again and again, not only from the pain but also from the sight of the grotesqueness of watching my lower body metamorphose into a giant fish.

When the transformation was over, I thought I died, as I was alone and consumed by darkness. I was at the bottom of the ocean floor where I waited in silence for a while. I was still trying to breathe through my nose and mouth, but all I did was choke.

After some time passed, my eyes adjusted to the dark. I stared at the horror that was my lower half. I was afraid to touch the part of me that should've been legs until I could not see my bawbels or my Man Thomas.

I quickly dug my hands around the area and, luckily, the whole package was there, nutmegs and all, tucked in a flap and easy to pull out just as if I'd have to piss with a pair of breeches.

Cupping my bawbels in my hand made me feel better and I hardly noticed I wiggled my tail, but the small motion sent my entire body streaming through the water. I remember hitting my back against the sunken ship wall. It was the first time I felt the power of my new form. But that was not all that was in store...

"Poseidon heard the slave praying to end her suffering and the life of the captain who'd been torturing her," Athena continues as she tells her version of the story. "So, Poseidon struck the ship with a bolt of lightning, setting it ablaze. But the three men—the deckhand, the Captain, and the Master at Arms went back to save what they could from the ship, including the slave."

"But they drowned. Isn't that correct?" asks Shelley.

"According to the historical accounts, yes," replies Athena, "but according to your aunt, that's not the end of the story."

"Because they were turned into *mermen*?" Yanka laughs and flashes me a wink and then blows a kiss in my direction.

I grin back, but my attention turns towards Shelley. Her chin is down, but her eyes will not avert from the sea. She appears quiet and at peace, though I sense a tempest is brewing within her.

I conjure a soft, cool breeze and send it through her hair. She tilts her head and closes her eyes as the corners of her mouth reach towards the sky. She's enjoying it. If these other women were not here, I would replace that soft wind with my hands, but I would not be as gentle with her as a mere breeze. I would grab her the way a storm grabs hold of a ship's sail and kiss her until the space between her thighs became a whirlpool of wet mess aching to suck me in.

Shelley catches me eyeing her thighs. "He's not a three-hundred-year-old merman," she says. "For all we know he's a murdering homeless man."

"I'm telling you, he's not!" yells Athena. "Look at the coin," she says and she lifts it off her head to dangle it. "This thing is a doubloon of pure gold dating back before the American Revolution and is probably worth over a million dollars. Do you really think a homeless man would be carrying something of so much value?"

"Did you just say that thing is worth a million dollars?" Yanka asks as she stands up to get a better look at the golden trinket.

"Probably more," states Athena, fixing her glasses to keep a better eye on Yanka.

"And where did Blue get it?" asks Yanka.

Athena clutches the coin again. "Poseidon gave it to him. Rather than let Blue and the other two men drown, Poseidon not only transformed them into mermen as a reward for attempting to save the woman, but he also gave them powers. Together, they are Poseidon's trident—three mermen to control the seas. One can manipulate the water, the other can control the beasts, and the third?" Athena examines me as she had the first time we met. "The third can control elements of the atmosphere, like the weather or this breeze."

"It *has* been storming more than usual since Blue arrived. Let me see the coin," demands Yanka.

"No!" shouts Athena. "The coin is cursed. Poseidon did not take into account the curse the slave put on the men before he struck the boat. Since the captain did not rescue the slave woman when he had the chance, the mermen were forbidden from being rescued. They control the seas, but they are also death dealers and forbidden from walking on land. As the slave was tethered by chains and drowned, she tethered the trident of men to the sea forever. Yet, Poseidon pitied the men for at least attempting to save the wailing slave. He transformed her into a sea witch, so she could undo the curse befallen upon his trident. Heaven forbid a man should return to land to have women! Reluctantly, the witch gave each man a trinket from the treasures of the sunken ship and shackled each merman to the trinket with magic. If a woman could not only lay with each man but love him in his beastly sea form as well, he could give her the trinket and walk with her on land."

"So, if Blue gave Shelley his trinket or his coin, then why can't he walk?" Yanka asks factiously with raised eyebrows.

"Maybe Shelley doesn't love him enough," replies Athena very seriously.

Shelley chortles, "Why would anyone choose to be tethered to another human? Wouldn't he just choose to be a merman and live forever?"

"Look around, Shelley," replies Yanka. "There's no one in sight for miles. It's fucking lonely out here."

Shelley sighs. "My parents are out here somewhere." Shelley turns back to look at me. "You know where they are, don't you?"

I hint at nothing.

"Why did they find your hair on my parents' boat?" Shelley asks.

"I'm telling you," stresses Athena, "he's a merman, just like your aunt said and I'm sure he was trying to help them."

I push my chair towards Shelley as she marches away towards Athena and quickly snatches the coin, tossing it into the water. My heart sinks with the coin that is beginning to make its way to the bottom of the sea and a bolt of lightning strikes the water.

"You've got to be fucking kidding me!" cries Yanka.

"I knew it!" shouts Athena. "You *can* control the weather," she says to me and I nod.

"That's bullshit!" cries Shelley. "That's a coincidence," she smirks and stands up. "He's a fucking murderer and a loony, too," she asserts and starts walking towards me like she's about to kill me.

I conjure another bolt of lightning to distract her and she trips and scrapes her chin.

She gets up angrily and demands, "Where are my parents?!" Thunder cracks through the sky, but it doesn't dissuade her wrath and I fear the fire shooting from her mouth. "If you're a merman then you know, don't you?! You know what happened to them! You know *exactly* where they are."

"Shelley, calm down," Yanka implores, as she gets between us.

I don't like this or seeing Shelley in this condition. She looks exactly like her father and it makes me ill. I have to tell her before she hurts herself.

"Do you know?!" she asks grabbing a hold of my shirt.

I nod, *yes,* and Shelley strikes me. She hits me so hard in the face I cannot remember the last time, perhaps in some pub brawl centuries ago, when I was struck to the point my face is throbbing. I massage my jaw and can't seem to stop the clouds from swirling above as a storm stirs.

"Where are they?!" cries Shelley. "Where are my parents?"

I look to the spot where Shelley tossed the coin, to where the sea has swallowed any chance I have of ever winning her affection or of ever being able to walk again, and I point.

"They're down there?" Shelley asks and I nod. "They're dead?" she questions once more and I nod again.

Shelley's shoulders sink as she strolls towards the edge of the boat, but as she walks I see she has a faint smile. "You've seen them down there, haven't you? And they're together? Have they been together this whole time?"

I sigh.

Athena and Yanka are watching the sky in amazement as the clouds quickly clear and I bow my head. I cannot look at Shelley knowing I'm partly responsible, but she deserves the truth, so I nod once more.

I hear a splash and both Yanka and Athena are shouting Shelley's name. Shelley has jumped over the rail, but she's not in view. All I see is the white aftermath of her splash adjoining a circle at the surface of the water as more bubbles rise from below.

Shelley is indeed her parents' daughter.

14

SHELLEY

It's dark down here, but something about the darkness feels familiar. My boots are dragging me down and I let my arms float to the side as gravity pulls down at me. I don't want to look down. I don't want to look up, either. It will call me back to the surface. So, I look straight ahead.

I don't know why I did this, why I jumped in, but I knew if I did I would sink. Somehow, I knew my boots would yank me down as if they had already done so before though I never reached the bottom.

The bottom. It's where I feel like I belong. I have no family, have never been in love, and I just broke a guy out of prison because, if I'm honest with myself, there is an itty-bitty place in my heart that wishes he was a merman who needed my help, which is lunacy.

Ridiculous. I'm ridiculous. Wherever my parents are, I belong with them. I know it. I've felt it my whole life. Aunt Cora even said so. "Earth is to water as water is to earth," she used to say. "Let yourself soak in the pleasure of the sea."

So, I belong down here, except I'm not just going to soak. I'm going to drown or...be *eaten*!

Straight ahead, I swear I see something move. My heart starts pounding and I feel like I need to breathe as something is coming straight at me. It looks like it's picking up speed as it glides towards me in a side-to-side motion.

Holy fuck! I can barely see the whole thing, but I do see the inside of its jaws strewn with hundreds of jagged teeth coming to gnaw on me!

I kick my legs and try to scream, but I only end up gulping water. I keep kicking and my heart is throbbing. I need air so bad. *I'm going to die.*

The mouth of a shark opens wide and I stop to face my death. I pray the pain will be over quickly, but then I feel a yank on my arm.

My head and legs jerk wildly in the water and I feel the scrape of the shark's back fin across my legs. My arm is gripped tight by someone's hand pulling me, but I'm more worried about the fact I can't breathe. I grab my throat and kick my legs as hard as I can—the shark is coming back.

The hand gripping me lets go and I see its connected to the arm of a man with an enormous fishtail. The man swims head on towards the shark and punches it.

I swallow more water as the man punches the shark again, which seems to stun the massive devourer. With one flick of his fishtail, the man swims towards me and grabs my arm again. He pulls me swiftly into the deep. I feel like we are racing so fast, I can't keep my eyes open so I close them.

As fast as we are going, my heart is slowing. The shark didn't get me, but I'm still going to die. I swallow more water and the hand guides me into a structure of some sort as I hit my boot on the rim of the opening, which hurts, but I don't care. I pull the hand that is gripping me, pulling me, and I really feel like I'm at the end of my rope. *I need air!*

The man comes behind me and lunges me upward above water and I can breathe.

As I come crashing back down into the water, the man takes my hand and leads it to grip on something over the surface of the seawater. I pull myself up and take a big breath. Water gets stuck at the back of my throat and I cough. I take another big breath as my heart pounds again, trying to absorb the oxygen it was desperate for.

Wiping my eyes with one hand, I realize I'm in the dark. I cough again and the sound of my hacking hits a few walls and echoes back into my ears. I'm in a room of some type. I wait for a few minutes, but nothing stirs except the sound of ocean water knocking.

"Hello?" I call out except I'm not sure I should be saying anything. Perhaps I should not be trying to attract any attention—especially not from anything that might try to consume me.

It's pitch black and I have no idea which way is out. I'm dangling in the water, my boots still trying to pull me down, but my head is able to stay above the surface as long as I hang onto what feels like a beam. I reach up to grab the beam with my other hand and listen intently.

The rhythmic plopping of droplets resounds as ocean water continues to knock against the walls of the underwater space. I'm not sure what I am in—an old ship perhaps, but it's so dark I'm more afraid right now than when I first jumped off the boat.

"Hello?" I call out softly once more and hear a small splash. "Who's there?" I ask with a quiver. I recall the man who came to my rescue and punched the shark. *Perhaps it was the lack of oxygen that made me imagine he had a fishtail.*

A light below the surface of the water comes into view. It's a fish with another one right behind it and the room begins to glow. I'm relieved to have some light until I see a shadow underwater at the corner of the room not more than ten feet away moving towards me. It could be another shark ready to eat me or it could be the strange creature that is half a man that brought me here to be its next meal.

It pops its head out—it's Blue.

At least, I think its Blue. It has Blue's face, but when I look down, he has the tail of a fish.

I sigh. *Why am I not surprised?*

"This isn't fair," I tell him. Blue squints and cocks his head. "I was beginning to like the wheelchair and now I have to get used to the idea of you with a fishtail, instead."

Blue smiles that big beautiful smile of his and it lights up the whole underwater chamber.

"You still can't talk?" I ask.

He shakes his head.

"Did you jump in after me?"

Yes, he nods.

"And your tail grew back?"

Yes, he nods again and reaches out to touch my cheek with his thumb. The feeling is comforting and I wonder if he has any kind of mystical power, which he might later try to use on me to seduce me like sirens so he can eat me—or so I've been told.

"Are you planning to turn me into a meal?" I ask and Blue slaps the water and rolls his eyes so far up into his head it makes me feel silly for asking. "It was a fair question," I say and he chuckles. "Are you magical?" I ask.

Blue's eyebrows crinkle at the center. He's thinking hard about it, but then he points to me.

"Me?" I question with a chuckle. "You think *I'm* magical?"

Blue nods and I laugh so loud, the vibration bounces off the walls in every direction until Blue wraps his hand around the back of my neck and kisses me.

The wet surprise of his lips on mine forces me to let go of the beam I'm holding and I fall into the water. I'm waving my arms wildly, but Blue grabs a hold of them, pulling me up, and helping me to reach the beam with both hands so I'm dangling again with my head just above the water.

Blue moves my wet hair out of my face. "You can't do that!" I blurt and wipe my face with one hand. "You can't surprise me like that."

Blue bites his lip, bows his head, and floats backward. This action surprises me, too. I don't want him to be so far away.

I speak softly. "I meant you can't keep scaring me."

The space between his brows crinkles again. He's confused and floats even farther away. The distance pulls at my heartstrings—*I want him closer.*

"Blue," I say in all seriousness, trying to get a grip on the fact that I'm attracted to him, "you looked like you were about to attack me in the hospital. Then you took a dive off the stairwell, and just now you popped your head out of the water frightening me because I didn't know what kind of creature you were. Plus, you kissed me out of the blue and without warning. You're a little unpredictable."

Blue's face sinks below the surface of the water, so only his eyes are showing. I can't help but speculate he dipped himself under because he doesn't want me to see him upset.

You're scared and now you're scaring him. Fix the flame in your mouth and stop messing this up, Shelley!

I adjust my hands holding onto the beam to get a better grip. "What I'm trying to say is I wish we could communicate better so I wouldn't have to be so nervous worrying about you and what you're thinking."

Blue's whole face floats back up above the water and he glides towards me leading with his hands like he's reaching for me, which makes me uneasy. I feel so vulnerable, dangling like a fish on a hook deep in his lair. As he comes towards me, I wish he could speak. I wish he could say what his intentions are.

Each droplet of water on every corner of his face illuminates from the glow of the underwater creatures below as he closes in on me. I'm not sure what I'm going to do if he tries to kiss me again and then I feel the bulk of each of Blue's strong arms wrap all the way around my back and squeezes as he buries his wet face in my neck.

He's hugging me. I can't remember the last time someone hugged or squeezed me so tight. It must've been my mother or father—they used to squeeze so tight I couldn't breathe. But the lack of air felt good in a way. To be held that tightly made me feel safe and secure. To be held *this* tight almost feels like home.

A sliver of an animal slips across my bare legs and I can't help but jerk my lower half and yelp. I kick the animal and Blue grunts as he lets go of me, looking at me with a crooked face.

I tilt my head down and I see it's him. It's his fishtail that got me feeling squirmy. "I'm so sorry!" I cry and he looks like he's pouting. "This is just going to take some getting used to. You know?"

Blue nods with a devilish grin and leans far back into the water to splash me in the face with the fan of his fin.

"Hey!" I exclaim as I dangle with only one hand and wipe my face with the other.

He laughs at me so I splash him back, but I hardly throw anything at him. He uses his hand like a wall against the surface of the water and splashes me again. I try to get him back, but my one hand slips and I sink underwater again.

I kick with my boots and Blue grabs my wrists and pulls them once more to the beam where I grip a hold with both hands. I feel his hands grip the beam, too. When I open my eyes I see we are both hanging, his face in front of mine. His lips are glistening wet along with his arms and shoulders while the rest of his body is hanging, leaning against me and I against him.

I feel like I can't breathe. My chest is heaving though my lungs expand so I know everything is working, but the thought of his wet, bare chest against mine makes me weak. I take in as much air as my body can possibly hold and blow it right back out, right into his open mouth.

He opens his mouth a tiny bit wider as he inches it closer. I know what's coming, so I close my eyes...

The soft pressure of his chilly wet lips sends a tingle through my core and I kiss him back harder. I sense Blue let go of the beam and dip slightly downward. I don't want his lips to part from mine, but he quickly swims back up and wraps one hand around the back of my neck as the other grabs my waist.

I grip the beam firmly as Blue tilts my head with his hand as he slips his tongue into my mouth kissing me again. His fingertips move across my belly and down between my legs as his fishtail brushes against my inner thigh.

"Wait!" I say and I pull my face away. "What are we doing?!"

Blue entangles his fingers at the back of my hair and grips at my scalp, pulling my hair to force my eyes to look straight on at him. He stares me down without flinching. Except for the ocean, which is causing us both to sway slightly, he doesn't move.

I understand the look he's giving me and I get what he's implying, so my lower jaw is trembling when I dare to ask, "Can we do that? You and me? Can we—"

Blue grabs a hold of the front of the waistline to my

shorts with his other hand and yanks me towards him. I bang against what feels like a hard rod at my groin. *I guess we can.*

Blue tugs again at the waistline of my shorts. I don't say anything, but I know he's asking for permission, so I take a breath and nod.

I watch Blue dip his head below the surface and tug at my boot. My feet become weightless as he takes one boot off and then the other. My jaw starts trembling when he slides his hands up my legs to my waist where I feel him messing with the button then the zipper to my shorts.

Looking around the underwater room, there's no sound except for the creaking of walls and soft knocking of seawater against each corner. It's peaceful, that is until I feel the sliver of Blue's tongue along the slit between my thighs and I want to let go of the beam, but I clench my hands tighter to hold on.

Blue rubs his tongue up and down on my clit and I *thank God* this man can stay down there without air. Blue glides my legs open, placing them over his shoulders, and I see tiny waves moving along the surface of the water from the turbulence of his swirling head rotating between my thighs below.

My body tenses as his head swirls faster and I slip, accidentally letting go of the beam. I slip below the surface, entangled with Blue, but he quickly grabs my wrists once more, pulling me back up to the beam.

Blue lifts my top and we both struggle to get it off. He ducks his head below the surface where his lips find my nipple and he licks and nibbles. I realize he enjoys me naked, vulnerable, and dangling from the beam like a fish caught on a hook.

Blue pushes my legs open again and grabs my hips as he pulls his body up and pops his head out of the water. I feel his lower half move between my legs and I don't know what to make of the sensation of a man that is not completely human but half of something else.

Grasping my hips, he stares me down again. Falling water droplets slowly run down his beautiful face and he enters me. The friction of the water seems difficult for him to easily glide in until his tail flicks and he thrusts himself deep within me.

"Ah fuck!" I cry. I tilt my head back, taking in every inch of him. With each thrust, I gasp as each bang of his animalistic power enthralls me. Using the water as leverage to maneuver himself, he grips and pulls up on my hips with his hands to plunge deeper and deeper.

My gut aches, but it's not just a physical pain. his carnal, robust actions make me want him. I want to be with him, to stay with him or he with me—in the ocean or on land, I don't care where. My heart aches for him and I want to wrap my arms around his lean, muscular build.

My gasps turn into moans and I grip the beam more firmly. With one of Blue's hard thrusts, I yelp—this time from the physical pain as my pussy engulfs his length and he floods me with his cum. The force of his seed feels like a drug taking over my body as I explode with pleasure.

The euphoria makes my body immediately go limp as I lose hold of the beam and sink below the water. Blue scoops me up and within seconds we are out of the submerged wreckage and surrounded by blackness. I can feel the power of Blue's fishtail as he propels us upward until we reach the surface near the beach house.

I come up to take a breath as my feet find the sandy bottom and Blue dive's back down into the water, but he doesn't come back up.

So, I wait.

After a few minutes, my teeth chatter from the cool night air blowing against my naked body. *Has he left me?* I turn my head searching for any sign of him, but the only things visible are the stars in the sky. I call his name though only the whispers of shallow waves as they crash along the beach respond.

I walk up the beach and seat my butt on the sand facing the ocean—my merman has abandoned me. *Merman.* I close my eyes and wrap my arms around me as a warm breeze passes over me, stimulating my skin and penetrating into my soul.

Blue pops his head out of the water and swims as far as he can towards me then drags himself the rest of the way up, spreading my legs, then getting in between them. He lifts the coin in his sand-covered hand and I'm smiling as he places the chain over my head and around my neck.

"Hey!" cries a voice.

I turn around only to be blinded by the flashlight pointed at me as Pike comes towards me. I hear a splash and look back to the ocean. Blue has made it safely back into the water when I feel Pike pull on my arms.

"You're coming with me, missy!" Pike yanks me up to standing. "Why the fuck are you naked?" he asks me. "Are you turning into a loony like your mother?"

I say nothing as Pike moves the flashlight up and down, not once, not twice, but three times.

Now, I feel exposed.

"Where's the stranger?" Pike asks as he starts to handcuff me. "This isn't a joke, Shelley. I know it was you and your friends who helped John Doe get out of prison. I get you all feel sorry for him, but helping a prisoner to escape is going to put *you* in jail for a long, long time and I'm not going to allow you to use any insanity pleas to help you."

I have no idea what to say as Pike pushes me towards his police car. My feet stumble through the sand and I turn around, barely making out a dark silhouette of what *might* be the top portion of a person, hopefully Blue, bobbing up and down in the water and making an occasional splash.

He's not clearly visible and I really have no idea if it's him I'm actually looking at, but my heart tells me to *believe*. I know I'm looking at a merman.

15

BLUE

*J*ail. That's what the sheriff said. Shelley is going to "jail" for a "long, long time." *Fuck!* At least she has the coin. I'm sure they will take it from her, but she has made claim to it. If it stays on land, I'm sure I'll be able to walk. *But what good is walking if Shelley cannot walk with me?*

Three hundred years ago, I would've thought Shelley was an aristocrat, changing her beliefs at any given moment to suit her needs. She's a bit of a brat, but it makes me want her more. She feeds those old desires, wishing to have been born with better status when I was a boy and a seaman. When she accepts me, those desires will be appeased and my status will no longer matter. Whether I'm a cripple or half a fish, Shelley accepts me.

I also know how crippled Shelley feels, having lost pieces of herself with her parents' deaths—something I have to fix for I am responsible. I just can't believe the one person I chose to trust with my fate is the same one whose life I already shattered—and I'm doing it again.

I have to help her, to save her, but a storm will not do her any good. My powers are made for destruction and a jolt of lightning or a flood of rain could hurt Shelley, along with many others.

My eyes follow Shelley as the sheriff accompanies her, in shackles, to his car. Lights flash, swirling like magic, and my stomach churns. *Magic.* I know what I must do.

Diving back into the deep blue sea, I swim for hours. By the time I approach Lenora's plateau, the home of the tortured slave turned sea witch, the sun has risen.

The sea witch's plateau rises from the ocean floor like a steep, snow-capped peak except it is flat at the top and rather than snow is covered in fine white sand. The plateau glows with a shimmering luminescence from the sun's bright light penetrating through layers of salty water. here, the ocean does not appear as the dark tomb as I know it to be, though this place *is* a tomb.

Hovering over the plateau, which is not much wider than a whaler's ship, I search for a way to wake the witch. If I could call out to Lenora I would, but my throat was scarred from the explosion on the night Captain Willis, Master Mayhem, and I tried to rescue Lenora and I'm hoping she can fix it.

I swim closer to the plateau and glide over it, skimming the fine sandy surface carefully for any sign or method of waking Lenora. The top of a single, rusted chain link comes into sight. I slip my finger through it and pull hard. As I do, a longer chain is exposed so I follow it, grasping the chain one hand after the other.

I find it leads back below the sand next to a toe whiter than marble. I yank the chain firmly, lifting the foot of a man shackled to the chain.

The toe and then the foot stir before a knee pops up. Fingers, as pale as the appendages, protrude and wiggle. Soon, an entirely naked man rises.

He's an Englishman and must be as old as me, as he's still wearing his peruke. I'm sure it's the only thing Lenora allows her captives to wear to feel the full brunt of their punishment. The white wig serves as a reminder of their social class, which has no bearing down here.

The Englishman stands then bends over and grasps at the chain linked to his other ankle and pulls, but that chain is shackled to another ankle. Another man rises who doesn't look like he's from my time. He's is as pale and powdery white as the Englishman, but his round features and short, kinky hair make him look like he is composed of mixed ethnicities. He has letters or numbers tattooed on his face, among other symbols, most likely etched into his skin in the last decade for his gang to identify him.

As the second man stands, he, too, pulls at his chains. One by one men rise from below the sand like corpses rising from the earth. Except these poor souls are not corpses. these souls are trapped in their own bodies—half-alive, half-dead. When the last one of at least a hundred miserable half-corpse men rise, they all gather at the center of the plateau before kneeling and bending over like dogs to dig their hands into the sand, digging for their master to awaken her.

Slowly, the sea witch rises from her sandy seabed. First, one dark hand emerges then an arm followed by the rest of her beautiful voluptuous body, which is a stark contrast to the men—pale and naked, each one linked to the manacles binding their thin bodies to her. I cringe at the shackles she wears—the same ones we found her in on the ship, which we could not free her from and nearly led to our deaths.

"Well, hello Henry," says Lenora.

I haven't heard my name for centuries. I always thought I'd cry if I should ever hear it again, but I'm distracted by Lenora's giant melon-sized bosoms swaying weightlessly in the pit of the ocean as she walks gracefully towards me with each one of her captives cowering at her feet. Her pretty plum cheeks flush as her enormous brown eyes get beady as she smiles at me, knowing I've come to her for help.

I point to a few of the new men she's captured and added to her collection.

Lenora huffs. "The slave trade is not what it used to be, but I've managed to collect a few more traders in the last century." Lenora looks to the Englishman. Her smile is gone and she cocks her head. I notice her hair is still tied in the same braided bun she's worn for centuries. The Englishman rushes as fast as he can through the water, paddling like a dog, and gets down to kneel behind her. She sits on him.

I gulp. As the master of wind, rain, and atmospheric energy, I have no powers down here and Lenora knows it. If she should choose to make me one of her half-dead slaves, she could.

I decide to cut straight to the point. I jab at the center of my bare chest.

Lenora laughs, "Yes, I've heard. Gossip travels fast underwater. The sea nymphs are as bad as humans when it comes to spreading the word on others' scandals. So, you've found the one who you think will break the curse and I see you've given her your trinket."

I swim down and wiggle the chain link that is bound to one of the men and then hit my wrists together.

"Yes, I know," Lenora says. "I'm already aware your lover is going to jail."

I clasp my hands together, praying to Lenora to help me.

"Help you!" Lenora laughs. "Help you to do *what?* Rescue your lover from the chains that will soon bind her, like the ones that bind me?"

Lenora bends to the side and tugs at the chain anchored to a collar around the Englishman's throat. His tongue is crimson as it pokes out of his pale white face and he gags.

The sight is quite repulsive. I can't imagine what it must be like to be enslaved to another. I rub my forehead with my palm.

"I'll tell you what, Henry, the wannabe hero and illiterate deckhand who thinks he was born of too low a status yet was never a slave."

I bow my head. Lenora is mocking me and she has every right to.

"I will make you a deal," she says, "because the truth is this girl—Shelley, the seashell, does love you. She loved you the moment you first pulled her from the water. It was simply misfortune for her to have forgotten what you did and credit another. Of course, it's been a wonderful comedy for me, but I don't believe a woman should be in chains for the sake of a man, particularly not a *mer*man," Lenora chortles. "So, here is my proposal."

My heart starts racing, not just with the confirmation of Shelley's love, but also because I knew this was coming. I knew Lenora wouldn't just help me. I'd have to make a deal and there'd be some price to pay.

"Since your lover has chosen to make claim to the coin," speaks Lenora, "I will help you. Your legs will be fully functioning and I will give you your voice back—for two days, but you must profess your sins to her. The child that lives inside of her is still chained to the past and she will never be free if she does not know the truth about her parents."

I close my eyes and nod.

"If the tender child she's buried inside decides to come out of her shell and forgive you, I'll let you keep your legs per our original agreement. If she chooses *not* to forgive you, you must return to the sea as a merman, never walking the land again. You will be chained to the sea as I am, as her parents are, and as her past is for all time."

The words echo in my head but I open my eyes. I

shouldn't hesitate with Lenora, so I nod once more in agreement before trying to swim away.

I suddenly feel a sting around my waist and turn around to see Lenora with the handle of a whip in her hand—Captain Averill Porterman's whip, the device of the man who tortured Lenora and many slaves.

She pulls me back and I notice each of the pale corpses have a small, devilish grin on their faces. "Magic is not free," says Lenora. "If you want your voice back, you will have to pay."

I squint my eyes at her and show her my hands, as I have nothing to pay her with.

Lenora stands up and pulls the whip so I'm face-to-face with her. "You must give up your power. The part of you that makes you a piece of Poseidon's trident, you must give it to me."

I shake my head. I know what the sea witch is trying to do. She cannot bear to live under Poseidon's rule. if she possessed the powers of the trident she would not only command the seas but possibly Poseidon as well.

The witch points to one of her slaves who brings forth a knife. I feel like I'm suffocating though my gills are working. I recognize the cutlery—it's the same knife Shelley's mother used to cut herself.

"As payment for the voice you plan to use to save your beloved little sea shell, you must cut yourself. As a merman and in this domain, you are too much like a god, Henry. You must forsake yourself and cut out the part of you that makes you imperishable. But once your blood leaves your body, your power will flow with it and I will collect it, then your power to control the atmosphere and the weather will be mine."

I unwrap the whip from around my waist. The sea witch

has never been a vile person, except to those who probably deserved her wrath.

"Think of it, Henry," she speaks. "You will have all you've ever desired—legs, a voice, a woman to rescue. You will not only be the man you always wanted to be but a hero in the eyes of the woman you love."

The witch is right. I'm not giving up anything but power over death and destruction. If Poseidon should choose to punish me, he simply will not be able to do so. I'll be on land and safe with Shelley, far from the sea.

I think about my two brothers and consider why they have not tried to intervene. Surely, they know everything happening, but they have yet to show themselves or attempt to stop me. I wonder if they would make such a deal.

I look into the witch's big brown eyes and hold out both hands. Lenora takes the knife from the man in chains and places it in one of my palms. As she retracts her hand, I see the scar in the shape of an "L" where she was branded by a hot iron so the world would know her status—*slave*. Lenora has endured more pain than any creature should bare and I feel humbled.

I think about Shelley.

I look at my hand and cut it. blood seeps into the water like lava flowing down a mountainside. The half-dead corpses start to waddle towards me and I choke. I flick my tail to create some distance and Lenora starts laughing. *I can't breathe.* I flick my tail harder and swim as fast as I can up toward the surface.

The sun is straight overhead and I propel harder, holding my breath until I finally breach into the open air. As I come crashing back down into the ocean, my body feels different— my lungs, my neck, my throat. I'm thrilled as I come back up to the surface to take a breath. Tomorrow, my legs will return and I won't just be able to walk to Shelley but *talk* to her.

"Shhh...Shhhell...lee."

My voice sounds different. It's been too long since I've heard myself speak. I flick my tail as I lay on my back. The sun's rays are beaming on my face.

"Ssssssu...uuun."

I tilt my head back just a little and see the flat horizon with no land in sight. Dark, heavy gray clouds are swarming in the direction I need to go.

I'm ecstatic to hear my own voice, but I'm more concerned with how I'm going to get to Shelley. I only have two days and, without gills, this is going to be a long swim back to Porterman's Bluff.

"F...f...fffuck."

16

SHELLEY

"Where did he go?" Pike interrogates me. It's the second day in a row and I admit it was not fun sleeping in a jail cell.

"I don't know what you're talking about, Sheriff," I say trying to keep my cool despite the fact the only clothes they could put me in was a tight, red, stretchy miniskirt and matching tube top probably leftover by a hooker.

"Goddamnit, Shelley!" Pike yells slamming his hands against the hard-cold surface of the metal table. "This isn't a joke! And if I didn't know your family's history of mental issues, I'd—"

"What are you talking about?" I ask. "What about my mental health? I'm not crazy!"

"You broke a man out of jail because you think he's half a fish."

"What?" I ask trying to sound surprised, although I *am* a little surprised. I'm betting it was Athena who could not keep her mouth shut.

Pike slams his fist on the table. "I don't know what the hell is going on in your head, but I really thought the whole merpeople bullshit was over with when your aunt died. Now, I got two women believing in mermen and I'm starting to think this whole John Doe...prison break...all of it, is some kind of hoax you've been planning."

Bitches! They *both* confessed and although it's the truth, it does sound crazy.

Pike leans in closer over the table of the interview room and stares me down. "I'm telling you right now, Shelley. I liked your aunt. She had a few loose screws, but she was harmless. It's also unfortunate we were never able to find your parents and I can only suspect that type of loss can really mess up a kid. But I don't like being made a fool of, especially as the sheriff in my town. I don't care how gorgeous those fair, long legs of yours are or how lenient I should be to someone who probably has some type of inherited psychosis, but I'm not fucking around when I say I want the asshole who probably took advantage of you on the beach then likely hit you to make you forget about it and now has you so confused you're willing to strip naked and lie for him! I'm telling you," says Sheriff Pike as he walks around the table and yanks my chair hard to face him that I nearly get whiplash. He puts his irate, flushed face in front of mine as he grabs the handles to my chair, flexing his biceps under a short-sleeved gray shirt until his veins bulge, and he snarls, "You need to come clean and tell me the fucking truth, right now!"

The heat of Pike's breath enters my mouth and I swallow. "He's a merman."

Pike sighs as he rubs his hand over his gaping mouth and stands upright. "You really should be ashamed of yourself, Shelley," he says, relocating his hands to his hips, making it hard not to notice his gun. "There's so much about this guy that points to something not right about him. Plus, there's evidence of him on your parent's boat, so I don't understand how you can protect him. Don't you want answers?" he whines.

In truth, I had forgotten. On the boat, Blue acknowledged he knew something about my missing parents, but I was too captivated by the allure of Blue's mysticism and mysteriousness after he rescued me from a shark, not to mention from myself, that I didn't get the chance to question him about my parents.

Pike leans down over me again, allowing his veins to bulge once more as he grabs onto the handles of the chair. His hot breath blows across my face, but this time his eyes are studying me. He looks at my forehead then follows my cheeks down to my chin before his eyes dip down to look at my breasts.

I cough and he looks me back in the eye. "I can see why your father was so in love with your mother. I knew she was quite brilliant, but he stuck by her side after she lost her mind. I think he loved her even more then." Pike sighs as he studies my face one more time. "I can see something is going on inside that pretty little head of yours and it just makes me so damn curious," he says licking his lips.

There's a knock at the door. "Sheriff?" asks the deputy, poking his head in.

The sheriff stands erect, keeping his eye on me. "I told you not to disturb us," Pike replies.

"I think we may have found our John Doe. Some zoology students were tracking and tagging sharks outside of the bay and say they spotted a man swimming naked towards shore. From their description, I believe it's our guy."

"Get up," says Pike, grabbing my arm. "I'm going to get to the bottom of this, so you're coming with me."

"She's not going anywhere with you," says a tall, husky black man with a bald head and round belly, which he uses to barge in through the door.

"Ah, fuck," Pike curses as Darius Grady, who is not only the public defender but also the only lawyer residing in our town, sits in the chair across from me causing Pike to growl. "What the hell are you doing here? Have you been tracking police business again with all your radio gadgets?"

"No!" Darius exclaims with wide eyes, which makes it obvious he's lying and he opens a folder then begins to spread documents across the table. "I'm here to see my client, who you're going to release because you have no reason to keep Shelley here. In fact, I recall seeing the two of you together at the Booty Festival the other night and I can't help but feel suspicious about the intentions you have with Shelley Morae." Darius clears his throat. "I mean with *the prisoner.*"

"Damn it, Darius!" shouts Pike.

"Boss," interrupts the deputy. "We gotta go if we want to make sure we get this guy in our custody before someone else does."

Pike looks at me and shakes his head. "Fine, Mr. Grady. She's free to go, but make sure she understands she's not allowed to leave town and if anything happens to her, she's your responsibility."

"I'll take good care of my client, Sheriff. Thank you very much," says Darius, winking at me.

Pike and the deputy leave and I fix my chair to face Darius, but he doesn't say anything. I watch as he stacks each of the papers he spread out just a moment ago. I'm so confused as he places the papers back in the folder and I notice his palms.

"Wait!" I say and reach forward to grab Darius's hand, pulling it to me and opening his fingers to look at his palm. "You have the mystic's triangle in your palm. It means you're a witch, but it's upside down."

Darius gives me the oddest, most inquisitive look. I hesitate and force a fake laugh. "My aunt taught me these crazy things. She tried to teach me to read palms. It's ridiculous, right? Hand reading?"

"Honestly, I'm intrigued," says Darius. "What does it mean if the triangle is upside down?"

"I don't want to insult you," I say trying to laugh it off.

"You could hardly do such a thing," laughs Darius with me. "So, tell me what it says."

I try to smile pleasantly as I report what I see. "It means that if you *are* a witch, you deal in the dark arts and—"

"You sound a lot like your aunt, Shelley. Next thing, I bet you'll be telling me I'm in disguise," Darius laughs, but I'm not laughing because that is, indeed, what I was about to say.

Plus, Darius has an odd laugh. it's rather high-pitched and almost sinister, more like a witch's cackle.

"I thought you didn't believe in all that hocus pocus," Darius continues. "You know, this isn't the first time I've had to come down to the station to bail out a member of your family for behaving like a crazy person so I highly suggest you keep these things to yourself." Darius stands up and as he grabs the folder, and I notice a scar on the outside of his hand in the shape of an "L" that looks more like he's been branded. It matches the brand on the slave drawn in Athena's book, so I lean back in my chair to create some distance between us.

I hear a crack of thunder pierce through the sky as Darius speaks. "You're free to leave, Shelley," he says and looks at me with bulging eyes. "Unless you'd like to stay, but I'd hate to see a good woman held captive for no reason against her will. That's a true crime, don't you think?"

Thunder cracks overhead once more and I nod in agreement.

Darius allows his big round belly to lead him out the door and as he leaves, I look at my palms. there are three spaces in my lifeline running from my middle finger down to the center of my wrist. Three times, my lifeline says I would come near death. The scrapes I have are near healing. I figure those are from the first time, which I can't remember, but I did end up in the hospital and I know it has something to do with Blue. The second time must've been the time Blue and I faced the shark. Nevertheless, the third time is yet to come and something tells me Blue is going to be involved in that somehow as well.

I stand up and glance down at the outfit I'm wearing and laugh at myself. I'm a lot older than how I am depicted, but I'm dressed as I am in Aunt Cora's painting, *Catch of the Earth*, that hangs in the beach house. She made sure I could always see it, even in the mirror if my back was turned towards it. The psychic old bitch made sure I'd always see myself in a teensy red tube top and skirt as she predicted.

And *I* predict it's time to go catch that fish.

17

SHELLEY

I head towards the sheriff's office receptionist and I
hear a tapping. The sound is coming from behind
a closed door and transforms from a tapping to a knocking.
Soon enough that knocking becomes banging and the door
flies open.

In truth, I'm really not surprised to see Yanka fall out of
the closet and land on top of the deputy, both of whom have
their pants down.

"Yanka, I need your car," I tell her.

"What the hell happened to you and Blue? And what the
fuck are you wearing?" she asks with a bug-eyed face. "You
all disappeared and the second Athena and I made it back to
shore, we were arrested. Then Darius, the public defender,
showed up to get us released and—" Yanka looks down and
smiles at the deputy, who smiles back.

"I got it," I tell her. "I don't need those details, but we do
need to get to Blue before the sheriff locks him up and
throws away the key."

Yanka reaches down to pull up her tight leggings. "How
did you all survive down there? After you both jumped in,

neither of you came back up. We waited for hours. We thought the two of you must've drowned or got eaten by a shark. I didn't believe a word of anything Athena was spouting until the deputy told me they found you. Now, I'm not so much a skeptic, but tell me the truth. What happened?"

"What happened is everything Athena said is true and we need to go save Blue."

The deputy, struggling to pull up his pants and red from embarrassment, proclaims, "You can't go after John Doe—"

"Especially dressed like that," says Yanka sarcastically.

"Will you focus, Yanka? Where's Athena?" I ask.

Yanka brushes her blonde hair back with her hands into a ponytail. It's a sign. she's going to help me. "Athena already took my car," she says.

"Listen to me!" shouts the deputy as he tucks his shirt into his pants. "The sheriff is on a rampage. He didn't even take me with him because he's got it in for John Doe. The sheriff doesn't want anyone standing in his way when he goes to collect the stranger. And if this stranger you all keep protecting gives the sheriff any trouble in any way, the sheriff is not going to hesitate to drop some heavy shit on John Doe's ass."

"Take us where the sheriff is headed," I tell the deputy.

"No," he says, "I'm already in enough trouble from John Doe's escape. There's no evidence pointing to the three of you, but I know you all had something to do with it. That was my responsibility, so I have no doubt I'll be out of a job soon and living on the street like our homeless stranger or a lost dog."

Yanka's eyelids flutter. "If that's really the case, you can always stay with me."

The deputy turns red again. "I can?"

"Sure," Yanka replies. "If you'll be out of a job with nowhere to go, I'd be happy to take you in."

I roll my eyes and interject. "Yes, Yanka will be happy to take you home when you become a stray dog, but you have to help us save Blue first."

"I don't know," replies the deputy, fidgeting with his holster.

"If you help me and Shelley, I'll take you home *tonight*," Yanka wantonly adds.

The deputy glances down at Yanka's enormous tits. "My car is out front," he says.

Before we leave, I stop at the front desk to collect the coin, which was placed in a large yellow envelope, and we get into the deputy's police car headed towards the coast. The three of us each take note of the approaching storm as lightning flashes, illuminating the gray sky at half-second intervals. The patrolman's radio cracks in loudly, alerting us to the sheriff's actions.

"Deputy, this is dispatch. We have a 10-24 suspicious person on scene near the marina and a 10-50 sheriff needs assistance. Do you copy?"

The deputy picks up the radio. "Copy that dispatch. Report sheriff's status."

"Possible 10-1 officer in distress. The sheriff is failing to acknowledge radio contact. Do you copy?"

"Copy that, dispatch. I'm headed to the marina now." The deputy hangs up the radio. "Listen," he says to us, "I don't know what's going on, so when we get to the marina, you two are going to stay in the car."

"You mean we *three*!" I say and point out the front windshield.

We glare out the window at Athena off the side of the road waving her hands as a flurry of gray smoke wafts from Yanka's car up into the sky.

The deputy pulls up to her and as Athena gets into the backseat with me, it starts to rain.

"What the fuck did you do to my car?!" cries Yanka.

"I didn't do anything!" Athena whines. "It was struck by lightning while I was inside and to be totally honest, I would think you'd be more thankful I'm not *dead*."

Yanka rolls her eyes as the deputy presses on the gas.

"And what the hell happened to you?" asks Athena, squinting her eyes at me. "What's in the envelope and *what* are you *wearing*?"

I open the envelope and allow the coin to slip into my hand as I yank up the red tube top.

"I was right, wasn't I?" asks Athena. "He's exactly what I said he is."

I look at her ebullient face. I don't know what she's seen or what more she knows about merpeople, but this is the moment she's been waiting for her whole life. I know what it means to want the truth, to have validation for the things you believe.

I grab Athena's face in my palms and look her straight in the face. "Yes. You were right."

Athena closes her eyes. A single tear drips from the corner of one eye leaving a salty trail down her face and into her mouth where I know she can taste the evidence bringing her closer to her lifelong conquest. She takes my hands off her cheeks and reaches for the coin then slips the chain over my head. "You have to keep it on," she says. "Don't ever take it off," she mutters and I nod.

There's something more that happened to Athena, which motivates her. It is something beyond a possible sighting of a merman. There's something going on with her, but as I'm about to ask her the deputy brings the car to a halt.

"You three stay here. You understand?" the deputy

instructs, throwing on his hat and skipping out into the pouring rain beneath crackling thunder and lightning.

We gather towards the center of the vehicle to see if we can get a look beyond the fogging windshield painted with images blurred by heavy rain.

"I can't see anything," I say and get out of the car. Within seconds, I'm soaked. Rain flies about in every direction—down over my eyes, up into my nose, and sideways to spout in my ear.

I hear men yelling and I run towards the sound. Running past a fallen tree, I can't believe my eyes. Blue is diving in and out of the water next to the sheriff's car, which looks smashed in the front and is half under water. The deputy is frantically skipping about up to his knees and pounding at the glass with the sheriff, who looks to be unconscious, inside.

I sprint down the sandy steep slope of the marina's borders where tire marks are left from where the sheriff's car slid off the road, over a pier, and into the water. When my feet reach the water, they feel heavy and I can't seem to walk or swim fast enough, even with all of the adrenaline pumping in my body, towards the front of the sheriff's car facing the beach.

Lightning strikes the ocean not far from where we are and I hear a voice yell at me. "Go back! Go back, Shelley!"

My heart stops—it's Blue. He's made his way onto the hood of the car. He's naked, using his legs, and *yelling* to me.

"Shelley, get back!" shouts the deputy who has managed to climb up to the hood of the sheriff's vehicle with Blue. "Get back!" the deputy warns Blue. "I'm going to shoot the window."

Blue dives into the water and the deputy pulls out his gun, firing into the windshield. The glass crumbles into thousands of pieces as water begins to seep in.

"Fuck!" the deputy cries out, reaching through the open window trying to free the sheriff. Blue gets back up on the hood and both men are frantic, attempting to wrench the sheriff free. He's clearly stuck as the car takes on more and more water as it sinks.

I watch in horror as the car goes down until the deputy is treading water with only his head visible. I swim out to him.

"Shelley! Go back to the car," shrieks the deputy as his head dips beneath the surface to look for the other two.

I plunge my head under, barely recognizing the silhouette of the vehicle and Blue's body—he's still trying to free the sheriff under the water.

Coming back up to the surface, the fresh rain mixed with the salt water fills my eyes and mouth. I take a deep breath and then clamp my mouth as I try to swim down to the car. Swimming as low as I can get, I realize it's too deep and swim back up.

The deputy, hardly able to stay afloat due to his uniform and boots, yells, "Ah, fuck!"

"They're both still down there," I tell him. "We have to try again."

"Go back to the fucking car!" he cries and, although I cannot see his tears mixed with the rain, his face is so wrinkled I know he's crying.

I duck my face back down into the water, but this time I cannot see them—no sign of the vehicle, the sheriff, or Blue.

I pop my head back up above the surface of the water as both the deputy and I tread next to one another. Rain pours straight into our eyes. I close my eyes and take one more breath of air, as much as I can hold, and dive into the water again.

I use every bit of kick I can to propel myself downward until I see Blue. Swimming towards him, I see he freed the sheriff so I help pull the sheriff by his collar, dragging him with me as I kick us both towards the surface.

As soon as I pop up, the deputy takes a hold of the sheriff, talking to him as he swims the unresponsive man back to shore.

I put my face back in the water, but I don't see Blue. I try to swim back down again, but I'm so exhausted I can't. Reaching the surface once more, I just breathe.

I take a moment. I look up at the gray sky then look back into the water. I still don't see him. I can't find Blue.

On the shore, Yanka performs CPR as Athena and the deputy watch. I should swim back to them, but I don't want to. I look for Blue once more, then I look to the open sea and swear I can hear it calling me. It sounds like my mother is calling me as she had often done when I was little to come play with her. Everything I've ever had any feelings for is out there.

As I lift one arm to swim towards the open ocean, a voice asks, "Where are you going?" I turn around to see Blue's head above the water. "Land is this way," he says.

18

HENRY

*a*dding another piece of driftwood to the fire, I poke at the mound of woven timber that crackles as tiny pieces of burning red cinder float into the evening atmosphere.

This was my idea. Shelley tried to kiss me the second she saw me in the water, but I couldn't allow it, not without telling her the truth first. Per the arrangement with the sea witch, I have to confess everything to Shelley and I need to do it before the sheriff wakes up and tries to take at least one of us off to jail.

Yanka was able to revive the sheriff and Doc says he'll be okay, which is great news, but I'm sure the lawman will be looking to hang someone for all his misfortune and humiliation.

As Lenora stated, if Shelley forgives me, she and I will be able to live out our days together as human beings. if not, I will be cursed to the sea for all time, minus the gifts Poseidon bestowed me.

Shelley's upset and indifferent towards me because I

ignored her advances. She even tried to hold my hand as the deputy drove us back to the beach house and she almost kissed me when she helped me learn to use the zipper on these denim pants, which are sewn together by rivets and are rather too tight and stiff to be comfortable. I do like the many pockets, which must be the only reason they are so popular and I enjoyed when she stuck her finger in one of my pockets.

"Talk to me," she said, but I couldn't. I just wanted to enjoy her company, at least for a few hours before the truth about her parents is revealed and she will likely leave me.

I could take her right now. She wants me and, by the gods, I want her, too. She's as in love with me now with legs and a voice as she was on the beach the first time we made love and I was only half human. She has not questioned my transformation, so I've chosen to do right by her. I've elected not to take her so she will not be disappointed to have given herself up to the murderer she suspects I am. Instead, I suggested we sit together so I may profess my sins, receive my punishment, and release her from the pain she's been carrying of never knowing what happened to the pieces of her that were lost at sea—her parents.

Thus, here we are beneath the stars and cloudless sky on a blanket on the sand next to a warm fire.

"You know what happened to them," she says. "Tell me."

I throw the stick in my hand into the fire and scoot back next to her. Glancing at her one more time, her face is full of determination and wonder, just as it was the first time I saw her ready to brave a mountain and not more than a day ago when I took her beneath the ocean. Her green eyes are like emeralds in the light of the fire and her hair glows red. The second I speak, I know that gem of a face might forever become lost to me.

"Tell me," she says again.

"I killed your father. He was as mad as your mother and at his request, I dragged him to the bottom of the sea where he drowned."

Just as I had suspected, the face I love is gone.

"I don't understand," Shelley says bobbling her head, lost in confusion. But she doesn't leave my side, so I try to explain what happened as I recall the events...

BLOOD TRICKLED into the water causing a frenzy among the creatures of the deep, but it wasn't the woman's blood that attracted me—it was her wailing. When I arrived, I knew immediately there was something wrong with her, something erroneous with her mind. Now I'm aware this was a result of the poison called mercury, as Athena explained.

The woman, Shelley's mother, was alone, but she could not stop talking to herself as she cut herself. She was beautifully dressed in a red gown fitted over skin as fair as Shelley's though she had thinned long blonde hair.

I feel guilty knowing now it was Shelley's mother. I found her amusing at the time, up until a man with fiery red hair, Shelley's father, showed up. He rowed himself to where she was and the second he climbed on board, she gazed at him and slit her own throat.

She fell into the water and I summoned the lightning to strike the beasts of the sea so they could not make a meal of her in front of the man who obviously cared deeply for her. Shelley's father took note of me, but he was not as shocked to see me as the few who have before and tried to escape. Instead, he dove in and, of all things, he could not swim.

It took every ounce of strength I had with my two arms to pull him back onto the bigger boat as he fought me. That son-of-a-bitch kicked and punched me until I was so sore I had to let him go.

He dove back in, but by then, his wife sunk to the depths of the ocean.

"Help me!" he cried. "Take me to her."

All I could do was shake my head, *No!*

"Please, you don't understand. She's my wife. I swore to her I would never leave her. Please take me to her. I cannot bear the thought of her alone."

I pointed at him and then into the water and wrapped both hands around my neck so he understood what I was gesturing—he would drown and die.

"My friend, there is a reason why you are here at this time and this place. There is a reason why you are in the shape you are in—you are here to *help* me. If I should die, if I should drown down there with the woman I love, you will not be responsible. I absolve you of whatever sin you think you will be committing. I forgive you and may whatever god or gods in our universe exist hear me say this: you must not only be forgiven, but *rewarded* for the act of love you are about to carry out. Please, I cannot wander this earth alone without her."

I knew how it felt to be alone, to be without companionship. I ruminated, but I decided to take him. I took him to the bottom of the sea to be with his wife, who was already drained of blood in the eternal tomb of the ocean.

I watched him caress her dead face and hold her lifeless hand as he swallowed with heavy gulps, the salty sea, allowing it to fill his belly and keep him anchored beside her.

At that moment, I felt more alone than ever before. I had lived without affection or any kind of human contact for nearly three hundred years, so I prayed to Poseidon, to any god listening, to perhaps help me find a love like that one day. I, too, would give up all I had—immortality and power, to receive such a reward.

I feel a hard smack on my face as Shelley strikes me.

"How could you do it?!" she screeches in my ear and I turn my head to see her face look as lost as her father's did on that dreadful day.

Shelley strikes me again and climbs on top of me trying to choke me, this time looking as mad as her mother.

Shelley hits me a few more times, but I take every blow until she starts to sob and lays to rest on me. I roll us over so I'm top of her and kiss the chubby part of her cheek smeared with salty tears streaming down her face.

She stops crying and just stares at me. I don't move or say anything. I've saved her twice, but I need her to save *me* this time. I need her to forgive me.

She lifts her head, closes her eyes, and puckers her pretty pink lips against mine.

I change my mind. I don't give a fuck if she forgives me. I'm taking this moment like it's the last one. Just like Shelley's father couldn't let his wife go, I'm not letting this moment with Shelley get away either.

I wedge my knees between her legs and it dawns on me— I'm about to take her like I haven't been able to before. the way I was meant to, as a man.

I get up on my knees and take my shirt off. I watch Shelley lift off her dress. She's got no undergarments on. she was hoping this would happen. We *both* wanted this to happen.

I reach for my button and undo the clasp and Shelley gets up to help me with my zipper, pulling down each pant fold. She pulls out my Man Thomas, taking it into her mouth and sucking on it. I run my hands through her strawberry blonde hair and watch her engulf me. It feels too good and I'm close to reaching my peak. I haven't had a woman suck on me for centuries and, as much as my Man Thomas would love to ejaculate in her mouth, I'm not ready for that yet.

I pull her by her hair and push her back onto the blanket and admire her. She's so soft, so fair. There is so much I have yet to discover about her as if she's a new found land. I want to run my hands over every peak and valley and make claim to every inch of new territory.

I rub my hands over Shelley's inner thighs. She smiles and trembles simultaneously. I stand to slip off my pants and remember thinking—*dreaming*, I'd run like a madman for miles if I ever got my legs back, but I'm not going anywhere.

I get on my knees, digging them into the sand and wiggle my toes to wedge them for leverage. I slip a finger along the slit of Shelley's privities, which she removes the hair from and I find different, but whatever makes her comfortable is fine with me.

She's wet. She's so fucking wet and I want to taste her. I dip my head down and take a lick as she moans. I lick the upper, small nub between her slit and her legs shake as she gasps.

I reach up with a hand to grab her plump breast and massage it as I stroke her most pleasurable knob with my tongue.

Shelley grips at my hair. "Fuck me," she says. Her eyes squint as they peer down at me. "Blue, fuck me."

I stop, getting up to lean on her. Her hands run over my chest, my sides, and scratch down my back. I lie on top of her and whisper in her ear. "Henry," I tell her and I slip my hard cock into her.

She hitches and closes her eyes.

"Henry," I say again and thrust deeper.

She moans.

"Henry!" I snap in her ear and I fuck her. I fuck her so

hard, her body is jerking from the force of my thrusts thanks to my legs.

I grip one of her legs to pull it up over my shoulder and she finally croaks, "Henry!"

She gasps as I get deep and she curses then bites my shoulder. This is the fire in her, the part of her that can be all-consuming but I need her to come back to earth. I still need her forgiveness. If I want to keep doing this to her—just like this, in this way with legs as a man, I need her to tell me I'm absolved.

I slow my pace and grab her by the chin to turn her head to face me. "Tell me I'm forgiven."

Shelley opens her eyes.

"Say my name and tell me I'm forgiven," I say again.

She sighs, "Henry, can we forget about everything that is right and wrong with the world? Can we forget any debate about whether the earth is round or flat and all the mystic and magic? Can we just be two people—you and I, a man and a woman, making love as we were meant to on this romantic beach?"

I bite my lip. That's not what I need but I nod.

"Just make love to me, Henry," she pleads.

I push myself deeper inside of her and recognize the irony of our situation. I needed her that first time we made love on the beach. I was only half human, but she fully gave herself to me. Now, *she* needs me and I need to give myself to her completely.

So, I toss and turn her, folding and bending her as I wedge myself inside of her, always making sure she feels everything I have to offer—my lips, my tongue, my hands, my strength, my manhood. The spark of her flame ignites with a fury, forcing her to come on my cock, and I extinguish myself inside her.

My legs are weak as I lay on my back and Shelley tucks

herself into my arm and at my side. I grip her tight as I stare up at the stars. In the morning, I won't be able to speak. The magic will be gone. I should be encouraging her with words to forgive me so I'll still be able to walk, but no words escape my mouth.

Tonight, I was a man who made love to a woman, which was all she wanted. Tonight, I believe I was a hero.

19

SHELLEY

I run my hand over Henry's chest. The fire burns low and a soft wind blows over our naked bodies, chilling me. The sound of small ocean waves tipping over the sand and fanning across the beach stirs me.

My parents are out there. Deep down, I always knew they died, most likely of drowning, but I can't fathom the thought they did it intentionally.

I tip my head to look at Henry's legs. Even with a fishtail, he could have stopped my mother from killing herself. With all of his supernatural powers, he could've created a typhoon of some type to knock her off the boat and swim her to shore before she took a knife to her own throat.

Of course, there's also my father. I'm sure he was having a moment of weakness and despair, but Henry had no right to lead my father to his death.

"I cannot forgive you," I tell Henry.

He sits up. "What?!"

"I can't—"

"Ah!" Henry cries and clutches his legs.

"What's the matter?!" I shriek as Henry looks like he's in pain.

"No!" he yells and starts to wail.

Scales appear on his legs, popping up one by one like bubbles bursting over his skin. Henry starts wailing in utter agony. I grab his face and he screams again, pushing me away, as I hear his fibula and femur breaking and then crumbling into misshapen lumps of unnatural horror that illuminate under an unexpected beam of light.

"What the *fuck* is that?!" shouts Pike. I look up to see the sheriff holding his flashlight and he whips out his gun. "Step away, Shelley," he cries.

"Put the gun down, Pike!" I bellow to him as a second light beams on Henry.

"What in the world is going on?" the deputy asks as he also draws his radio to call for help then drops the radio to pull out his gun.

Henry leans forward, still wailing, as he tries to haul himself across the sand with his forearms towards the water.

"You stay right there!" Pike commands, pointing his gun at Henry. "I knew there was something fishy going on with you," he shouts.

"Stop it!" I say as I get up and run towards Pike to try to grab his hand and move his aim. "Henry saved your life, Sheriff!"

I see the deputy put his gun back in his holster. "Shelley's right, Sheriff. Whatever's going on with the guy, we should probably help him."

Pike pushes me off and snarls at the deputy, "I don't know what kind of crazy shit is going on in this town, but it's clear I'm the only sane person left!" Pike points his gun and flashlight at Henry. Henry's fishtail is completely intact and he's only a foot from the edge of the water.

"Stop right there!" yells Pike as he cocks his gun. "Somehow, you're responsible for Shelley's missing parents and I'm glad I came out here to check on Shelley because I'm sure you're after her too. I don't know what kind of devil you are and what kind of psychic bullshit Shelley's family has been cursed with but you'd better stop. Right there! Or I'll fucking shoot you."

Henry stares down the sheriff. His face is aglow from the flashlight making his blue eyes sparkle like gems. His tail glimmers under the moonlight. Henry scoots forward and I hear Pike's gun go off.

I'm screaming as I run towards Henry when another shot resounds through the shadowy seaside. I feel a stabbing pain in my arm, but I keep running to Henry whose face is down in the water and he's not moving.

"Henry!" I call to him and flip him over. He's choking on the water and sand in his throat. I prop him on my lap and hold him. I hear the deputy and the sheriff scuffling in the background along with sirens approaching, but I block the noises out of my mind.

Henry reaches behind his back and brings his hand forward. Despite the dark of night, we can both see and smell blood trickling over his fingertips from a bullet hole in his back. I start to cry and squeeze him tighter as my arm stings. Pike shot me too, but I believe it's only grazed my arm so I'm okay.

"The sheriff is right," Henry says. "I think I could've saved your mother and all I did was drown your father. I'm responsible."

"That's not true," I say.

"I'm responsible," he says again as I begin to sob. "I never meant to let you live with all that pain—never knowing what happened to your family and chained to your past for so long," says Henry.

Steps approach in the sand. "What the hell?" screeches a

man in the company of a woman. They're dressed in black and white uniforms and carrying a stretcher.

"He's been shot in the back," I say.

"Yeah, okay. Let's get him on the stretcher," replies the woman, as if she's completely unfazed by Henry's fishtail.

The paramedics struggle to carry Henry, despite my help. He's too long for the stretcher and, thankfully, the deputy comes to help us. We load Henry into the ambulance, but they won't allow me to go with him. They say Henry is hardly responsive and they're going to need all the room they can get to work on his wounds.

The deputy pulls a blanket from his car for me. I forgot I'm stark naked so I wrap myself up. As the ambulance siren gets farther away, I hear the sheriff in the back of the deputy's car pounding away at the glass like a crazy person. the deputy locked him in there after the shooting. I do feel a little sorry for Pike. I know what it's like to be deemed crazy.

The deputy states he's taking Pike to the mental hospital to get the sheriff some help, which is fifty miles in the opposite direction of where Henry is going. Then, the deputy says he's coming back to take me to the hospital to see Henry. He tries to reassure me Yanka will take good care of Henry as she was on her way to the hospital.

I watch the deputy drive away with blue lights flashing and within seconds, I'm alone.

Facing the beach, I skim my eyes across the vast ocean. Many times in my life, I wanted to get lost in that ocean to be with my parents and not feel so alone. Henry's right. I've been living chained to the past for nearly the entire length of my life.

"I'm sorry for you, Mom, and I forgive you, Dad," I tell them and I can't help but get the feeling they hear me. "I will bring Aunt Cora's ashes so she can join you. And I hope you will all forgive me because I'm forgiving Henry, too."

20

HENRY

*W*eeks later...

I don't want to read this book about green eggs, I tell Shelley with my hands. *This is a children's book. When can I read the book about the whale with big bawbels and a giant Man Thomas?*

"You're not ready for that book yet, Henry. And *Moby Dick* is *not* about a whale's big penis," Shelley scolds.

I close the book. In truth, reading is a lot harder than I thought it was going to be and I'd prefer Shelley read to me as she does sometimes in bed. Although it's not because I want to hear the stories. It's so I can grope between her legs while she's easily distracted.

"Listen," she says. The spark in her tone makes her sound annoyed. "If I had to learn to read your hands to understand what the hell you're saying, you're going to have to learn to *read that book.*"

I sigh. Shelley did not pick up on sign language as quickly as I did, so it was frustrating for her. I believe she had a hard time learning to sign because she was so easily distracted by a person's fate, which she picks up on whenever she sees a person's palms.

But she did put in the work with me. We made it through the full eight-week sign language course at the university, which Athena referred to us. Shelley's become an expert at reading hands and just as she has the gift of reading palms, like her aunt, she has acquired the gift of reading *me*, too.

I open the book back up over my lap to appease her and sign to her. *How long will you be gone?*

Shelley turns and tilts her head up to look at the peak of the mountain. I know she's nervous. Her aunt's final wishes were to have her ashes spread over the bay from the top of the lookout. This task is the reason we met and it's unfortunate she must still make the trip alone.

Of course, I'd go with her if I could, but the bullet wedged in my lower spine prevents me from walking. Doc, who grew up in this town and graduated from the nearby university, has a very open mind about everything that's happened. He says he doesn't want to remove the bullet for fear I could lose complete function of the lower half of my body.

Shelley grabs the handle to my wheelchair and leans down to kiss me. "Two hours max," she says to me and turns to her friend, Kumiko, who's stretched out like a starfish, covered in oily darkening lotion atop a picnic blanket. Kumiko won't climb the mountain because she despises Aunt Cora, but I genuinely wish I met the old woman.

"I'll be back in two hours," Shelley says to her friend. "You'll keep an eye on him for me, won't you?"

Kumiko seems perturbed as she tries to stuff the side of her breast back into her red bathing suit, which is hardly a suit and looks more like a harlot's undergarments.

"Where's he going to go?" Kumiko questions with sarcasm. "He can't go anywhere."

Both Shelley and I chuckle at the notion and I grab Shelley's palm and kiss it. *I love you,* I mouth to her.

Shelley reaches down to the coin around her neck, pulls it up to her lips, and kisses it. *I love you too,* she mouths back to me, and I watch Shelley adjust her backpack and start to make her way up the trail.

An hour passes and I'm finishing up my third children's book when Kumiko decides I might be worthy of conversation.

"Can I ask you something?" she questions.

I turn to see she put her dark glasses atop her head and is studying me with her beady eyes, which makes me nervous, but I nod in acknowledgment.

"How do you guys do it?"

It. I know what she's asking. Sex is not exactly what I thought Kumiko was going to inquire about, but I can see how someone might be curious. I shrug my shoulders.

"I'd really like to know," says Kumiko. "I mean I get why

my friend is so into you. You're hot and everything, but does your thingy still work?"

My eyes fly wide open. I'm sure she can read my face, but I nod with exaggeration to be clear she understands, *Yes!*

"So, does Shelley always get on top or," she coughs, "how do things maneuver between the two of you?"

I belly laugh because Shelley warned me about what a promiscuous little nymph Kumiko is, but I have no idea how to tell Kumiko the ways in which Shelley and I have sex. Kumiko probably wouldn't believe the half of it if I could speak and describe it to her.

Suddenly, I hear a scream. I look up and see Shelley tumbling down the mountain. This time, I know it's not my fault, but I do know which way she's about to shoot off the mountain and land into the bay.

"Holy shit!" cries Kumiko. "She's going to die—*again!*"

I push myself off my chair and start to drag myself to the water.

My arms sting from the hot sand and Kumiko is yelling for me to come back.

I stop at the water's edge and take off my pants. I'm pretty good with a zipper now and I scoot myself into the water. My legs hurt as they break and crumble then reshape and transform into a fishtail. I can even feel the bullet move in my back as I gain movability of my fin.

Kumiko is wailing at the top of her lungs at what she sees. I'd wish she'd be quiet. wailing wakes the gods, but I'll have to worry about that after I catch my lover.

Shelley goes flying into the air as she had once before, so I don't waste any time flicking my tail to torpedo through the water to catch her. I'm a little late as Shelley lands in the water, but I'm there to pull her up to the surface.

Shelley wipes her dripping wet face and I stop her hand

from wiping it a second time so I can kiss her. I love the taste of the ocean in her fire-breathing mouth.

You did that on purpose, I sign to her. *You were testing to see if I'd come to your rescue.*

"Well, of course," she says as she wraps both arms around my neck. "How else am I supposed to give you a reward?"

Shelley kisses me again, until we feel a disturbance—a wave, push from beneath us in the water. Shelley clings to me, wrapping her legs tightly around my waist. I laugh at the sight of a large purple creature, nearly the size of a barge, scud beneath us. I use the opportunity to kiss Shelley's wet neck and nibble on her ear, but she's too distracted to bite back.

"What the hell is *that?*" shrieks Shelley and I grab her bottom cheeks to pull her even tighter onto me then tilt my head sideways so I catch her attention, forcing her to look in my eyes and read my lips.

My brother, I mouth to Shelley and grin.

Shelley turns to Kumiko on the beach, who is wailing even louder as giant purple tentacles reach up on the sand.

Shelley sighs. "Maybe we should rescue her," she says but I just smile and sign back.

Oh, no. Trust me, she's exactly his type and my brother deserves a reward of his own. We'll let him save her.

End of Book 1

THE SEA MEN SERIES

Book 1: Lovers Catch
Book 2: Lover Peak
Book 3: Lovers in Deep

ACKNOWLEDGMENTS

Dearest Reader,

Thank you!

LOVE,
DANI

Your time to read, review, comment, like, and share means more than you could ever know.

To my DARC Team, my editor, the Bloomers, and all my reviewers, thank you so much babes!

xoxo,
Dani

MORE BOOKS BY DANI

American Badass
Bang Lords
The Fourth Knight
The Sea Men

Your free book awaits...
For more books by Dani and to view my other pen names,
Sign up to the Babe Fuel Books newsletter at
BabeFuelBooks.com.

ABOUT ME

Hi! Dani Stowe is the pen name for the author/creator of Babe Fuel Books. Everything you'd like to know about me can be found at BabeFuelBooks.com/about. But if you want a quick run-down—I like to sip on coffee, chai, southern sweet tea, and pretty much anything that promotes sugar and caffeine in a rich candied combo while I'm reading. I love to read.

Bookbub
http://bit.ly/2qgT7Oz
Facebook
http://bit.ly/2OSJ94k
Newsletter
http://bit.ly/2NxDtHu
Pinterest
http://bit.ly/2OU05rt

UP HER

BANG LORDS, BOOK 1

Preview
by DANI STOWE

Charlotte

One.

Just *one* kiss.

It was a soft kiss and a bit wet. Elliot licked his plump lips before he adjusted his glasses and then moved in cautiously to plant a soft smooch on my mouth.

That was twelve years ago and I'm still thinking about it —the *one* kiss. It was his reward and it was all he got for saving my life.

I sometimes wish I'd given him more. I fantasize about it. I'm fantasizing about it right now as I hustle through city streets to get some coffee before my first day on the job. I'm wondering *again* what Elliot might've looked like under those geeky glasses and preppy clothes. His eyes were pretty enough—a light brown like creamy milk chocolate. I wonder if they sparkled more than most brown eyes because of the glasses. I didn't wonder much about the rest of him, although I'm sure he would've shown it all to me if I'd asked him.

But he was a geek back then so it would not have been cool because that was twelve years ago and *that* was high school.

I remember the day Elliot saved me like it was yesterday. He and his two geeky friends, along with the rich boy, came busting in through the ceiling of my second story bedroom to help my three friends and me from being burned alive.

My house was on fire. It was my senior year and I decided to throw a party since my parents were out of town. The fire department declared it was the moonshine and burning cigarettes that caused the fire. By the time my girlfriends and I smelled smoke, flames had already come through the hall upstairs and we ran to my bedroom. We were screaming for help with no way out the window, as it was blocked by safety bars my dad installed when I was little to keep me from falling out.

Smoke filled the air and the four of us huddled at the window as heat loomed on our backs. We were screaming, pushing on each other hoping to break free of the imprisoned room when we noticed Elliot and his friends with a jackhammer, a rope, and a ladder. They extended the ladder from Elliot's house to mine and crawled like firefighters from one attic window to the next.

Elliot was my neighbor. We played together when we were little. He liked to show me his bugs. I liked to show him my braids. But as we grew older, my body matured while Elliot hardly did at all. He grew tall, but he was skinny— skinnier than most boys, even skinnier than me. His thin frame and high, round cheekbones under fair skin made him look like a starved baby and he knew it. So, he never shaved, but he hardly had any hair around his jaw. It was splotchy. I always wished I'd told him he *should* shave. He probably would've looked better and not like he was trying so hard to look manly.

I didn't have to try hard at all to look womanly. I was lucky to have blonde hair that I could grow long to match my long legs because I developed boobs early—nice ones, too.

When we got to high school we both got a lot of attention. I got popular with the *in* crowd. Elliot, on the other hand, became a popular pick for being *bullied* by the in crowd.

I never participated in any of the bullyings, of course, but I did tease him. I liked the way Elliot would glance at me from his bedroom window straight across from mine. Occasionally, I'd walk past my open window wearing only my underwear and the poor guy would break a pencil or choke on his milk, spitting it out all over himself. Elliot studied a lot at his desk, which was angled in his room so all he had to do was look up to see me.

Interestingly, I'd never seen Elliot without his glasses. I can't help but think he kept them on—*always*, just in case I was ever in view.

Looking back, I think I liked Elliot. I liked the way he was always spying to get a glimpse of me. Sometimes, I wished we had stayed friends, *but the bugs!*

Ugh, the bugs. I could never understand how he never grew out of that interest. Elliot's predilection for creepy crawlers seemed to impede his chances of ever having friends until...

Nick. Nick was Elliot's "rich boy" best friend who moved to town during freshman year and became the presumed leader of the geek squad known as *NIM.*

Nick was hot, smooth, and a definite bad boy, but it was obvious he didn't fit in with most crowds—too much of a rebel and, like his geeky friends, he was really smart. Not intelligence, but street smarts. Nick plucked each geek like he handpicked them out of *Lonerville,* and they all became their own little squadron of rebels—avoiding anything that had to do with high school except being present in class.

NIM hung out a lot at Elliot's house. For the most part, they were curiously quiet except when they were conducting their science experiments and blowing stuff up with a bang.

I always felt they were up to no good. It's not surprising Nick, Elliot, and the other two geeks now own a billion-dollar drug corporation, which they *also* named NIM, the Neuro Institute of Medicine.

I heard the geek squad lives lavishly nowadays. Rich Nick invested all his father's inheritance into furthering the education of his three geeky friends. Elliot became a biologist, Jax, a chemist, and Don—apparently, he's a sex therapist with multiple degrees in psychology. But it's my understanding they all have multiple doctorate degrees, although no one from back home has seen them since graduation.

Thinking back to the night of the fire, after four years of those boys being picked on in high school and us girls never stepping in to do anything about it, the last people I ever thought would come and save us from being burned alive would be Elliot and his team of geeks.

But days after graduation, my house and my party went up in flames and just when I thought I was going to die, NIM came. Three geeks and the rich boy rescued me and my girl-friends—Sue, Nancy, and Loulah. Loulah was Nancy's younger sister. She was a geek herself, but we kept her around kind of like a mascot. She ran our errands, did our hair, performed every dumb dare we nearly forced her to do, and pretty much just took all our shit.

I regret it a little bit. Loulah was a good girl and we treated her like crap. She had an infatuation with Nick. It was fitting for her that it was Nick who pulled her out of the fire, except she became his bitch after that day and no longer ours.

Loulah works for Nick now. She's always worked for Nick and, according to her sister Nancy, Loulah doesn't have any time to do anything else. She barely speaks for a minute on the phone—always consumed with the work Nick has for her.

As I walk through the city, I debate if this is really a good idea. Loulah called me. Over the last dozen years, I've bounced from job to job—nothing ever serious and most often getting fired for reasons I could never quite figure out. Layoffs. Budget cuts. *Whatever*. And I could never seem to keep a boyfriend. Anytime I got close to someone and things started going well, the guy would dump me.

It was embarrassing to return home a month ago to my

suburban town as the ex-prom queen with no job and no husband at thirty years old. I had to move in with my parents, but that's not the worst of it. *To see all my classmates happily married and with kids?* I just feel worthless, like a loser, like high school was the best thing to ever happen to me, even though it was fake. It was all fake because I was a fake back then.

When Loulah called, I assumed her call was also a fake. I thought she was pranking me, trying to get back at me for all the shitty dares I made her do as a teenager. But she was serious. She offered me a job at NIM saying Nick needed more than just one assistant and she thought it would be nice to have a friend to work with. I was surprised Loulah would call me, but then again Loulah never had friends other than us so I guess she didn't know what a real friend was and, I admit, I was a horrible friend.

I was hesitant at first to accept the job. I wasn't sure I wanted to face the geek squad knowing they all work there, especially since I didn't even thank most of them for saving our lives. Plus, the idea I might have to face Elliot, who probably lives in a mansion with his gorgeous wife and beautiful kids, makes me a little ill. But anything is better than living with mom and dad who remind me every day how I cost us our home, not to mention, I need to stop making excuses, grow up, and keep a job. I swear it just feels like the world is against me, like something keeps kicking me down on purpose.

As I skip through the crosswalk in my beige heels and a fitted, yet conservative, knee-length navy blue skirt with a cream button-up blouse among masses of other city slickers, I can see NIM.

It's a rather dark building—all glass with nearly black tinted windows. It reminds me of Nick. He was the one with dark hair and dark eyes—the *Dark Lord* of the geek squad. I figure since he was the guy with all the money, it's no surprise the building would reflect his persona.

My stomach churns as I approach the coffeehouse across the street from NIM. Facing people back home was hard, but I have no doubt facing these people—the people of NIM, the people of my past, will be harder. I tell myself that perhaps this is fate. This is my chance to start over, to be a good friend to Loulah, and to thank the people who saved my friends and me by being of service to them as an efficient office assistant.

As I reach to grip the silver handles to the large glass doors of the coffeehouse, I notice my hands are trembling. Retracting them, I take a look—I'm shaking so badly though I don't know why I'm so nervous. I stand there for a minute reconsidering whether I should get a coffee and croissant. The coffee might make me jitter more and the croissant could cramp my stomach. On the other hand, if I skip it I might faint later having used all my stored energy due to my anxiety. The last thing I want is to pass out on my first day of work.

"Let me get that for you," says a man with a nice melody in his voice.

I glance up to see an older gentleman, Asian, with faded jeans and a gray sports coat. He pulls the door open.

"Oh, thank you," I nod and hop into the coffeehouse, falling to the back of a very long line.

It seems like an eternity by the time I get to the front of the line and I'm about to open my mouth to give the barista my drink order when his attention gets diverted.

"Hey, Mr. Nine! The usual today?" he shouts to the back of the coffeehouse.

I turn to see the dark silhouette of a tall man against the bright morning light beaming in behind him through the glass. As he comes closer, I notice he's brawny and dressed all in black—a turtleneck with black slacks that is decorated with coordinated leather accessories—shoes and a belt that boasts shiny gold buckles.

The line moves to the side as he enters. They are clearing a path for him like he commanded them to move with the pure will of his presence. I gulp as he comes into view under the coffeehouse lights. His face is strong, tan, and bristled with a trimmed short beard that is as black as the slick side-parted hair on his head and the clothes he is wearing.

He cuts right in front of me. I know I should say something as he starts to place his order, but his smell—expensive and woodsy, makes my tongue hang. Literally, my tongue is hanging out of my mouth as he and the barista inquire about one another until they are joking. I am officially panting when he flashes a brilliant smile.

He glances my way, still smiling, and now I know I need to eat something because I already feel like I could pass out.

"Hi!" he says with unexpected enthusiasm, turning his whole body to me.

"Hi," I smile and realize I'm slouching so I stand up straight.

He looks me up and down, which is very odd and perhaps rude, but honestly, I don't mind he's looking, except I can feel the line of people behind me are gawking at us or maybe *him* for cutting.

"You know you cut in line, right?" I inquire. Surely, he knows but I just have to ask. I don't care how gorgeous he thinks he is.

He smiles, but before he can open his mouth, the barista is talking.

"This is one of the Mr. Nine's coffee shops."

"Mr. Nine?" I ask.

"What's the matter?" asks Mr. Nine. "You don't like the name?" He cocks a brow as he chuckles and I swear to God,

177

the cocky bastard is the sexiest thing I've ever seen since... since... *ever*.

"Hey," he tells the barista and points his thumb at me, "get her whatever she wants."

"Oh no, that's okay," I fumble to say. "I can pay for myself."

"I insist," he says with a low, gruff tone that quickly changes to a higher and strangely familiar pitch. "Do you want to sit down and chat? I don't know where you're headed, but—"

My cheeks flush. I drop my hand as I realize I'm fanning my own cheeks to cool off. "I probably shouldn't. It's my first day today."

"New job?"

"Yeah."

"At where?"

"At NIM. Do you know of the corporation across the street?"

Mr. Nine's brows furrow. His demeanor changes as I notice his Adam's apple bob beneath his turtleneck while he takes a gulp of air. He looks almost angry, angry with the mention of NIM and he turns to take the steaming hot coffee from the barista.

He blows the steam away with softly pursed lips before taking a sip and then turns back to stare wide-eyed at me with stark green eyes and a most serious face. "I work there," he growls, taking me by the elbow to lead me out of the line. "Who hired you?"

"An old friend of mine works there—Taloulah Berkeley."

"Hmm," he groans. "I should escort you."

It's unusual—his tone and the way he just handled me, so I grin. "I'm fine."

He takes another sip before asking, "So, you must know Elliot Crowe as well?"

The mere mention sparks a tingle in my chest and I shudder as I speak. "Yes, I know Elliot. I haven't seen him in a long time. Does he still work at NIM?"

"Oh yeah, he's one of the managing partners and a fantastic scientist, quite brilliant actually."

I can feel the corners of my mouth reach my ears. "I'm sure Elliot, or *Mr. Crowe*, is an exceptional scientist and probably more. He's really quite special."

"Is he now?"

I gulp as I nod.

Mr. Nine's eyes narrow. "Do you mean that or are you being facetious?"

I take a breath. I have no idea who this man is other than he works at NIM and owns the coffeehouse, but by the look of him, I have no doubt he's someone important.

I didn't have an interview and I couldn't take the time out to research the company. I had one day to pack, fly out here, and find the hotel, which NIM is paying for until I get my own place. So for all I know, this guy could be another one of the managing partners and I'm about to get fired because I'm behaving suspiciously before I even start.

I stand up straight and smile boldly. "Mr. Nine, I don't mean to be rude, but I really should get going. I don't want to be late on my first day and please, believe me, I have nothing but the utmost respect for all of the scientists and partners at NIM."

"Then you should let me escort you there. In fact, I'll take you exactly where you need to go."

Mr. Nine takes another sip of his coffee and puts his elbow out to me. When I first took sight of him, I do believe I would've dropped my panties if he'd asked me, but right now, I'm reluctant to grab his arm, which I do anyway because he says he knows Elliot.

He leads me out of the coffeehouse, passed the line of

gawking women, without responding to the barista who shouts, "Goodbye."

When we hit the sidewalk, my head tilts back to get a good view of the NIM building across the street and Mr. Nine takes my hand. It's awkward, but I let him squeeze my palm and lead me to play leapfrog through the street where there's no crosswalk between vehicles zipping by.

I try not to grip too tightly onto the man I just met, though he's gripping me like I'm his kid and he doesn't want me to wander off. I figure maybe it's a *man* thing and he *keeps* holding my hand as we cross the sidewalk to enter the sliding glass doors of NIM.

Inside is as dark as the outside. The décor is smooth, polished black marble. Business people are staring at us—like we are a couple holding hands inappropriately in a place of business and I try to pull my hand free, but Mr. Nine grips tighter.

"This way," he says and leads us towards the elevators where he finally lets go to click on a few buttons at a small computer kiosk that controls six elevators. One set of doors open and Mr. Nine reaches to take my hand again, but I tuck my arm behind my back.

I don't mean to be standoffish and I don't really care he's being so forward or that anyone notices us holding hands. But I do care that *one* person might see us. For whatever reason, the last thing I want is to be seen holding another gentleman's hand if I should run into my old neighbor and friend, Elliot Crowe.

ELLIOT

I can't fucking believe it. She has no idea who I am.

Get Bang Lords No. 1, Up Her

THE FOURTH KNIGHT

Preview
by DANI STOWE

RUE

Rue

He's watching me.

I drop my gaze. I do not want to draw suspicion.

Trailing my fingers along a heavy wooden table, I envy the spread of plump juicy fruit, charred chickens, and dribbling greasy pork ribs, but cringe at the boar's head—dead on a stick. The swine's tongue hangs thick and dry between its tusks. I notice a small pitcher filled with red wine nearby. I'd like to sip on it or, better yet, toss it right in the face of His Majesty and the man standing next to him, the man making me feel uneasy.

I lift my chin as the other ladies do, although I'd like nothing better than to stuff some of what's on this banquet table between my bosoms and legs to carry it out. This is enough food to feed an entire village. Sadly, it will be wasted and left to rot like our kingdom's people.

My gaze wanders up again.

Damn! The tall, masked man in black standing next to His

Royal Highness refuses to deflect his eyes from me. I look down at my golden dress, which matches my golden blond hair, and my bosoms are heaving out of my chest. I wish Adelard had stolen something a little less revealing.

Slipping between chatty women who have caught the attention of drunken men in fine clothing, the sour smell of aged sweat stings my nostrils. I pinch my nose together at the stinky nobles while chuckling at their conversations.

They are all in a game and behaving like animals. The women bat their eyes and play coy, while the men purse fishy lips hoping to catch more than kiss. I wish they'd just come outright and say what they're really after—a chase that ends with a doe bucking somewhere in a dark corner of the castle or outside up against a tree.

My blue eyes twitch as the man in black sways noticeably from the corner of my eye. I can't help but turn my head to him completely. He's broader in the shoulders than I'd originally noticed. His stance is straight and he holds his head high. He's overtly confident, even cocky he seems. I believe he's more than just another one of King Richard's soldiers. He could be a knight, though he's not dressed like one. Being in such close proximity to the king, it's possible he could be something much more.

I wish I could see his face. The thin ribbons wrapped and tied around our heads cut only to show our eyes hardly convey a mask. We all wear masks, except the king, being it's *his* party.

I study His Majesty's surroundings. Soldiers, armed with swords, stand by though I believe it will be easy to get past them simply because I'm a woman. The king will likely expedite my proximity to him when the time is near. The bastard has already allowed at least a dozen women to fall into his lap, including *girls* that have been forced to take a seat on his knee for entertainment.

But the tall man with short, cropped black hair adjacent to the king worries me. He does not cease to watch me. I suspect he is becoming suspicious, but worse, I suspect he might be my *tracker*.

I've never beheld the man, my tracker, a supposed hunter and, rumored to be, master swordsman. His recent appointment to hunt me, *the outlaw*, and kill me has been decreed. though he is lucky we have not crossed paths—*yet*.

Villagers say my tracker is growing increasingly frustrated—threatening to take hostages and throw them into the dungeon where they will be tortured to gain information about my band of skilled bandits. The coarse, trimmed beard bristling along the man in black's lower jaw certainly fits the description of the man charged to reel me in. If he should find me, I'm sure he would love to gut me—run me through.

I bite my lip to keep myself from laughing aloud.

I'm told if I should ever encounter the man tasked to track me, that I should run. They say he is a knight who wears no armor. His confidence in his skills with a sword proves he doesn't need the iron shielding. From this distance, I can see a shred of muscle that reaches from behind his ear down his neck and to the front of his collarbone. I do not doubt, it is the result of wielding a heavy sword.

I clamp down harder on my own mouth to keep ridiculous laughter from escaping. Unfortunately, I'm not a runner. I'm a fighter and no sword can match my bow.

I look to the man's hip. There dangles a hefty blade of unusual making. The hilt appears to be red, as if the jewels embedded within have been stained with blood. I contemplate how many wives the man in black has left widowed with a slash of that sword.

He will not make a widow out of me, I chuckle to myself. Luckily, I have enough foresight and skill to kill him first, *and* I'm not married because I don't have to be!

I look about the room to ensure I have an escape—I spy several. The front door where all the king's guests have entered is well guarded and another door stands behind the king, although I don't know where it ends. My final destination may be a window. If need be, I will pull at the banners hanging from each side, toss them over the ledge, and climb down to my good friend, Adelard, waiting with our horse. From there, we will ride back to the safety of the forest.

My eyes gloss over the king again, bringing the man in black to take notice. I gulp. He is quite a specimen. He behaves more like a guardian of sorts. If I should be struck down once I kill the king, at least I will die happily knowing I got the best of *both* men—one murdered for revenge and the other bested with embarrassment.

Oh no! The man in black bends to his side. He's whispering in the king's ear while he continues to keep his eye on me. He points his finger behind his back straight in my direction. *Dear Lord, I hope I have not intrigued him.*

My stomach churns. I might miss my chance to follow through on this deathly plot. *Perhaps I should make my advance now?*

Damn it! I knew it! The man in black comes my way.

As he approaches with long, bold strides, I feel for my dagger tucked into the long sleeve of my dress at the wrist. I look past the man coming towards me to the king and my heart sinks. If I cannot assassinate the king, I will at least execute *this* man. Tracker or not, he is someone of value to the king and once he's dead, he'll be of no further threat to the other outlaws.

"Excuse me, my lady," he says with a smile. He bows and I curtsy as Adelard taught me to. "Forgive me, but I do not seem to know you."

I feel for the bottom edge of my knife as I examine him from head to toe. He's much taller than me, but the perfect height to *stab!* With a simple flick of my right wrist and a hard jab, the handle of my dagger will slip into my palm, allotting me the opportunity to quickly pierce the flesh of his belly. By jerking the sharp tip upward at an angle after penetrating the cavity of his soft torso, my dagger will slice through his bowel and he'll die a slow, painful death.

The curves of my mouth float upward with such thoughts, though I really wish he'd go away.

His lashes flutter at my smile. *Damn! Do not give yourself away.*

"Should you know me?" I ask, wickedly.

He huffs and the wrinkle at his brow furrows deeper. "How did you arrive here? You do not sound or look as if you belong amongst this crowd."

My heart paces and I allow my middle fingertip to trace the handle of the dagger. "I am the cousin... of..." I fumble to speak, completely forgetting whom I'm supposed to be related to. I'm apparently to be an out-of-towner rumored to arrive for an arranged marriage. Adelard forced me to practice this part at least a hundred times because I've never been good matching titles and names.

"I am the cousin of... De-el-la... Claaaa—"

The man smiles excitedly. "Lady Claire!"

My knees weaken when he places his hand behind my head, pulling me to him, speaking softly through my hair and into my ear. "I did not think you would be arriving for another week," he whispers, his warm breath tickling its way into my ear canal.

He's so close. His body heat is radiating.

So much for the stab to the abdomen. If I have to kill him, I'll stab him right in the back!

He moves my hair from my ear as he continues whispering. "The king promised me a suitable and fair maiden. Even with that ribbon concealing your eyes, you are lovelier than I anticipated."

Suitable? Fair? Lovely? I'd like to cut his prick off and see how *suitable* he'd think I am then. I'm sure he would no longer be suitable to *any* woman thereafter.

"Would you like to take a stroll outside?" he asks with hope in his voice.

No, I don't want to take a stroll outside! I'd like for you to piss off so I can kill the king!

I tilt my head sideways to look at him. His brows are raised—weak with anticipation, but the man most certainly looks mischievous and *dangerous*. Nevertheless, I do believe he thinks I am this woman he's apparently been waiting for.

I gulp. "I am not—"

"Am I being too forward with my future wife?" he asks.

Future wife?

Fine bristles of his hair lining his chiseled face brush against my cheek as he brings his face directly in front of mine to gaze into my eyes. In my twenty years of life, I don't think I've ever had my face this close to a man's besides my father's before he was murdered by the king's knights years ago.

The man in black dips his chin a little. The pungent smell of fine, fruity wine on his breath is overbearing. He stares blankly at me with deep green eyes that sparkle behind the slits of the black ribbon-turned-mask tied around his head. I am infuriated with the fact his eyes are quite chivalrous.

"'Tis okay to be nervous," he says, gripping my elbow and nudging me to follow him.

I stand my ground, unmoved.

"Come, my lady," he says. "I will not bite."

I look around. Guests are staring and beginning to gossip. I was not supposed to bring any attention to myself, thus I take a step in his direction.

As I follow my potential tracker, I look back at the king sitting gleefully on his throne. He's staring at us. Perhaps, if I endure a few moments with the man in black, he'll introduce me to His Royal Highness, allotting me the chance to stab the king—*dead*. As dead as the swine I reluctantly leave behind.

I am led out to a balcony where several people are about. My "suitor" seems disappointed. He rubs my fingers wrapped around his elbow with his palm. "We should go somewhere a bit quieter. I would very much like for us to speak in private. Would you mind accompanying me to the garden?"

He's raised his hand to present a cobbled path leading towards a landscape filled with botanical life and flower buds glowing under the full moonlight. The garden is pretty, trimmed, and tamed, unlike the forest. If I was not a wanted fugitive with a reward on my head, I might be inclined to think I'm fortunate to be led by such a handsome man with wealth and status to a romantic garden outside of a royal castle.

I nod and his face brightens. The man has a very wide smile that competes with the stark white roses in the background, dazzling like the stars above.

Poor roses. It's possible they will become stained a blood red should I have to slaughter this man out here, but I've always liked red roses better anyway.

The man leads me down the steps to a set of perfectly cut rectangular stones placed in a circular array. He gestures I sit, so I do as he requests. From the corner of my eye, I feel his gaze follow my face as I lower myself to sit on the stone. His gaze shifts towards my breasts and I cover my chest with a palm, feeling naked.

He flinches at my discomfort. "You will have to forgive me."

I bite my lip. *You're in the king's service. You don't deserve forgiveness,* I silently think.

"When I first saw you," he continues, "I could not help but think we have met before. You look strangely familiar. By chance, do you have those same feelings?"

I shake my head, *no.*

"You do not talk much." I shake my head again and he chuckles. "Would you prefer I remove my mask?"

I reach forward to stop him, as I don't want to have to take off *my* mask, but he's rather quick and slips the ribbon easily over and off his head.

A tingle runs through my chest like a cool breeze encapsulating me, causing my skin to tickle and gooseflesh to rise. *I feel even more naked at the sight of him.*

He does look familiar, but I'm not going to admit it.

"Perhaps, we should discard your mask, too," he says, reaching for my face.

I clutch his fingers. They are long and strong, but I grip them.

"Ah!" he cries out in response to the tight squeeze of his knuckles pressed bone against bone and he cocks his head sideways.

Surprised at my strength? You should be.

I push his fingers back to him where he presses my hands flat and firm into his chest. My cheeks warm as I retract my hands and he smiles once more to reveal deep muscular trenches to the sides of his strong upward smile. I can only imagine the lean cuts of muscle he must have spread across the rest of his body.

I admit it will be a waste to kill such a fine-looking man. I feel worse as he takes my left hand and kisses my knuckles with warm, moist lips. He attempts to pull at my right hand, but I feel the weight of the knife there, so I jerk my hand back.

He sighs. "I am sorry. We are not married yet and, considering your family history, I am sure you are a most restrained and reserved type of lady. I heard you are the only family your father has left, which is why he has allowed you to become as old as you are without being married."

I roll my eyes.

"I am not stating you are...mm...old," he stutters. "I just mean most young ladies are already made wives by thirteen or fourteen, some even younger. A few young men are even made husbands by such an age, but my work in service to the king has left me no recourse to take a wife—until now." He smiles again and I am forced to bite my lip for some strange reason. "I believe King Richard has finally taken pity on me, allowing me to marry. I shall reach my thirtieth year soon. I am glad he has found me a wife that is not so young."

I huff. *I want to kill him. Kill all of them!* The thought of girls being plucked so young infuriates me. To avoid such savagery is one of the few benefits of having grown up as an outlaw among orphans.

Oh no, my face has given my thoughts away. He attempts another kiss at my left hand, which I pull back but he will not let go.

"Do not let my commitment to King Richard cause you fear."

I'm not afraid! Do I look afraid?

He strokes my left hand with his thumb. "In all my years of service to the king, I have won many battles for him, captured and killed many an enemy and saved the king's life several times over. He is frustrated, for I have not seized the leader of the band of outlaws, but the task will at least keep me home, here, in the kingdom. I am sure you have heard of the resistance residing in the forest?"

A chill runs down my spine—*here sits my tracker with my hand in his.* I attempt to pull my hand back once more.

"Do not fret," he continues tugging my fingers into his lap. "I will be a good husband to you. I am close to capturing the leader and the king has promised me a small fortune for all my service."

I don't give a crap about fortune. I want my family back, you arse!

He runs the pad of his opposite thumb across my cheek. His finger is warm. My cheeks flush scarlet at his touch.

"I am sorry," he says bashfully, "I have devoted too much of myself. Perhaps I should not have been so bold to discuss knightly things with such a fair lady. I am certain you are not interested in men's business and bloody tales."

I bat my eyes. Regretfully, I admit it's not likely I will kill the king tonight, but perhaps I can escape with information. "I am interested."

"Are you?" his face brightens.

I fake a smile back. "Genuinely."

The man in black cocks his head again. "Lady Claire, I must admit, I am relieved. You are a breath of fresh air. I was hoping to choose a wife of my own, but the king would not have it. Sometimes, I deem he confuses me with being his brother, as we are so close in age, or even sometimes his father, as he has lacked one for most of his life. Arranging our marriage, I believe, was his way of rewarding me for pledging my loyalty to him for so many years."

Not to mention, you're also his number one marksman, executioner, and assassin!

"May I please remove your mask?" he inquires, reaching for my face, but I smack his hands. "Forgive me, Lady Claire," he murmurs as he rubs the sting. *I hope it hurts!* He scratches his forehead. "My feelings have been in a quandary as of late. I was excited at the thought of taking a wife, then fearful of whom she might be, not having the choice for myself. It has vexed me for some time." He examines me again with his sparkling green eyes. "Seeing you now, I must say I am most excited. I promise I will be a good husband. Fear not my behavior this evening. I may have appeared as unruly as the outlaws, or worse, untrustworthy. Will you pardon me for making so many untamed advances?"

Never!

"Sir Hale," calls a king's messenger from the balcony. "Our king has retired to his chambers and wishes to speak with you."

Sir Hale. I recognize the infamous name.

He nods at the messenger and turns back to me. "This is something that will be commonplace. Tis likely we will live in the castle with the king once we are married. I will be at your beck and call, second only to the king, I promise." The man is trying to sound cheerful, but it's obvious he is distraught with the thought. "Will you meet me tomorrow? Meet me at the market after the morning bell tolls. I would love to take you on a tour of our beautiful countryside."

I wish to laugh. In fact, it's taking an enormous amount of energy to contain the urge. It's I who should be giving the tour. No one knows these lands better than my gang of outlaws and me.

I grin, but he doesn't stand to walk away. He is waiting for definitive confirmation. I believe my chance to assassinate the king, along with the significant time my gang and I have invested on this night, has been wasted. But another plot ruminates in the back of my mind. Perhaps I could get this man to reveal things to me, letting me in on everything he knows.

I force a heavy nod in agreement. Sir Hale kisses my hand again, but as he gets up to peer down at me—my soul ignites!

I don't just recognize him, I *remember* him.

My mind shatters. I watch him turn away. He's still smiling as his right hand caresses the handle of his sword at his hip. I am filled with a rush of emotions. My heart and mind are battling one another with such ferocity, my whole body feels alight and I want to tear off this stupid dress to reveal myself.

I *will* meet Sir Hale tomorrow and I *will* make sure I am privy to everything he knows because I *know* this man and this will *not* be the first time Sir Hale has aided me.

HALE

There is something familiar about her, like she is something out of a dream or, perhaps, a memory. I prefer it be a dream. If I did not have to march my feet to meet with King Richard, I might take a moment for myself to allow my mind to wander.

"Lady Claire," I say to myself as I march through the castle. Her name rolls off the tip of my tongue. I wonder what she tastes like. I know I promised to be a good husband, but tis likely she is a virgin, as she should be, yet the thought of tearing her open and making her scream with her first feel and thrust of me is already driving me towards lunacy. Her scent, like forest lilies, along with the color of her lips, as if stained by red wine, are enough to make me hard and now I'm desperate to know what she looks like.

I should have torn that mask from her face!

I smile to myself. *Ah, who am I fooling?* I'd take her with the mask on. Hell, I'd fuck her with the dress on. I doubt she will have a chance to make it out of her wedding dress before I pull at her golden hair while flipping up her gown. I will not even have to slap her arse to get her to tighten around me—she is a virgin! She'll be screaming her first time, but it should only be the one time and I'll be a good husband after that—*maybe.*

For now, I suspect I should play the role of a gentleman and make it easy for Lady Claire to meet me at the altar. She will be my wife, after all. Perchance this is my one opportunity to know what tis like to have a family. Richard is the only family I have known, as my own was slaughtered when I was a child. Consequently, I am subordinate to Richard.

Some days, I think I shall allow Lady Claire to not feel as though she is subordinate to me. It will be nice to have someone I might be able to speak my mind with, someone I shall confide in. Lady Claire seems attentive to my words. I pray she was genuinely interested. Tomorrow, perchance, I should be more attentive to *her,* if she should choose to speak more.

I march faster as I enter the king's chambers. His door is wide open and I am not surprised to find three nude ladies in his bed with him.

"Sir Hale!" the king beckons to me as he scurries off the bed. A servant drapes him with a thick red velvet robe. I am thankful for the slight chill blowing through the windows, which forces him to cover up. I hate having conversations with him when his scrawny body is entirely exposed and his measly lanky cock is erect. He likes to admire it and I fear he should ever see mine. The king might remove it from me. Tis twice the size of his when standing at full attention. I have known the king to do barbaric things when he is jealous. Many a finger have been severed from hands he decided were too large, heads from men he thought were too proud, and daughters from fathers he deemed too pretty.

"Twas the young lady with whom you disappeared?" Richard continues. "I believe you beat me to her. I was just about to call her to sit upon my lap when you commented the need to fetch something at the banquet table. I had no notion you were talking about that fine specimen of a woman."

"Forgive me, Sire," I say and bow my head. "Lady Claire arrived early."

"Oh my!" shouts the king, cocking his head. He looks confused. "Was *that* the Lady Claire? I had no idea she'd grown to be so...beautiful!" He laughs at himself in the full-length mirror—admiring his curly blond hair. "Well, she did have the mask on. Were you able to take it off, Sir Hale?"

"Yes," I lie.

"And what did she look like?"

Get your copy of The Fourth Knight.

Made in the USA
Columbia, SC
27 November 2020